I0604282

Killer Is Me
THE BALLAD OF HANK KELSEY

This book was typeset using Apple Garamond, in Affinity Publisher 2, & designed by Jonathon Wolfer.

ISBN 978-0-9887989-5-3

For Claire & Atticus

Chapter 1

"I was born in 1674 on a farm here in the Connecticut Colony," Hank said flicking a brass Zippo open and closed. He had used it a few minutes ago to light the campfire and was now leaning back in a wooden Adirondack chair close to the flames on his farm in Kelsey Town. The fire crackled and smoked. It was a new moon and the sky was clear and full of stars.

"That's really how you want to start this?" Nick was laying in a hammock, he had the whole hammock stand right next to the fire pit, looking up at the constellations. Orion just peaked over the Eastern horizon for his journey through the sky.

"Why not?" Hank pulled a beer bottle out of the cooler sitting next to him and popped the cap off with his thumb as he snapped the lighter closed in his other hand.

"It's cliché. Might as well say you were born during the biggest blizzard of 16 dickety 2." Nick pulled his iPhone out of his pocket, and held the button down to turn it off.

"From what I am told. it was raining, but it was April. It rains a lot in April here," Hank said. "And do you have to be texting right now?"

"You're so thick sometimes," Nick laughed. "And I'm turning it off. Did you turn yours off?"

"I don't even know where that stupid thing is." Hank took a healthy gulp from his beer. "Where should I start then?"

"Start with when you were cursed, specifically the night your daughter went missing."

"I don't want to talk about that," Hank looked to the fire and the clank of the Zippo opening rang over the crackle of the burning logs.

"Fine, you were born in April of 1674, Continue."

"Now I don't want to start there either." The lighter clicked closed in his large hand.

"Let's start with whatever memory pops into your head right now then, go."

"Everything isn't in perfect order up here." Hank pointed at his head with the hand holding the beer, then took a sip.

"That's fine, whatever comes to mind. You just need to talk so I can see your memories, remember how this works? I'll figure a timeline out later."

"Yeah, you and your little ability to see inside my head. Well, the first thing coming to me happened when I had been around for over a century," Hank took a sip of his beer. "And it's a pretty terrible memory."

"I think I can handle it. You remember what year it was?"

"1836, maybe," Hank belched. "I had gone West, like many others in the age of manifest destiny. Many terrible things happened here because of my curse and I thought that going as far away from here as I could, that things might change. I was wrong."

Killer Is Me
Independence, Missouri 1836

Woke up in a puddle of blood.

It wasn't mine.

Some of it was already dry on my skin, but most of the blood was just a slippery mess all around me. Pushed myself up slowly, hands slid forward through the puddle, and my knees slipped back. Slammed back down on my face.

Dug my toes into the floor, carving an inch into the wood, giving myself a little traction. Then dug my finger nails in and pushed myself up to my hands and knees. Brought one leg up, rested a hand on that knee and looked around.

Light streamed in through the windows. The curtains were light, delicate and white making the room seem much bigger than it was. The wall paper was of flowers and the gas lamps were polished brass. The furniture was exquisitely carved hardwood and satin covered cushions.

"Damn it," I whispered. I knew someone was dead, most likely a few people. Had lost control, again. Just couldn't place who lived here.

I didn't.

Rose to my feet, smelling the air, but all I smelled was death. I looked into the gilded mirror and my face was covered in blood and my hair was matted down with it.

I stepped out of the puddle of blood. A wet sticky sound filled the silence with every step leaving behind bloody foot prints.

Left a trail as I headed to the kitchen. I could easily find my way back to the puddle of blood. No one could get lost following those tracks.

I had only come to this house for the first time last night, but knew where everything was. I had gotten the grand tour, before killing everyone.

Yanked the cloth off of the dining room table before stepping into the kitchen. Silver candle sticks and a few other knickknacks clattered to the floor.

The floor in the kitchen was slate, and it was cold. No one had tended the fire in that room, or any room, through the evening, and the brisk April night air of Independence, Missouri had crept through the house.

There was a wash basin with a full water pitcher in the center. I tore off a piece of the table cloth and wiped as much of the blood from my hands and face as I could. Then I filled the wash basin with water, and cleaned my face, hair and hands. Used the rest of the table cloth to dry off.

Upstairs, I found a closet with men's clothing and chose a nice dark grey suit that fit a little tight in the chest, but didn't need to be wearing it too long. I could get to my home before any of this was discovered, change and disappear. I'd done it before, and I'd do it again.

The house sat on an estate on the outskirts of Independence, Missouri. My home was only a few minutes away, but even on the outskirts the city was awake and buzzing with people getting to work, or preparing for the trip west to the Pacific. Independence had become the Queen City of the Trails, with paths meandering to Oregon and California.

No one paid me any mind as I walked through the streets, and slipped into my home through the backdoor.

It only took a few minutes to change into something more comfortable for travel, and I grabbed the bag I already had packed from the closet in the front hall. I had lived off of that same pack many times over the previous few decades.

There was a knock at the door.

I cocked my head at the porch, listening. Shook my head, walked over and opened the door.

"What?" I said, looking down at the boy standing on my porch.

"I was out collecting for the paper, Mr. Kelsey," the boy said.

Reaching into my pocket, I pulled out a few coins and dropped them into the boys hands. "Keep the change, you've been doing a good job. Not like other kids who toss the paper wherever they please."

"Oh, wow, thanks a bunch Mr. Kelsey," the boy said and ran off to the next house.

Stepped outside and closed the door behind me. I wondered if he would be the one to find the mess I left behind earlier. He was running that direction.

All I had to do was walk off into the wilderness, and keep going. I could find my own food, kill whatever I needed with my bare hands. But I wouldn't need to eat for a few days. Not after last night's feast. Just keep going and get away from people.

With the next step, a flash tore through my brain. Like a bullet tearing through the flesh.

A scream.

A step.

Blood running over my clawed hands.

Another step.

The thump of dead weight hitting the wooden floor.

My pace quickened.

The taste of blood in the back of my throat.

A glimpse of my tusked head in the blood splattered, gilded mirror. But only snout and teeth, then neck.

I was running now.

The mirror hung in the drawing room of the woman I was calling on that evening. We had been growing close, and I let my emotions get the better of me. Felt drunk with the feeling of love and lust and the touch of a woman's hand in mine and forgot what day of the month it was.

Her name was Lucy Devereux.

She was dead now.

Her servant was named Emma May.

She was dead too.

Now I was running faster than any human could, but I was in the woods.

The memories wouldn't stop.

None of them were in order though. They never were when I lost all control to the moon.

In the mirror, in Lucy's drawing room, I felt myself stoop down and saw the image of a giant, pink, tusked pig head looking back with my own eyes.

In the next flash I was gnawing on a femur, crushing it in my jaw and drinking down the marrow. Could feel the warmth of it as though the marrow was running over my chin and down my neck and chest that very moment.

The underbrush was thick, but I cut through it easily and so quickly that only maybe a few raptors in the sky could register my movements.

Every step crushed leaves and sticks and ferns beneath my boots. And every step shot a memory through my head of a chew, or a chomp, or of blood running over my fingers.

Three peoples' worth of teeth grinding together, reducing them to fuel. My fingers tearing pieces off as though they were well cooked chickens.

Mile after mile, the memories filled in leaving the previous evening clear and crisp.

This had been happening to me for almost two centuries, but it didn't always hit me so hard. I was usually so careful, sending myself away for the full moon as far from people as I could get. But I had let loneliness and despair get a hold of me, and now those I sought out for comfort were gone. The change was always worse when my emotions were running high, when I felt most alive, when I was in love. That is the point to the curse.

Lucy was dead.

Her father was dead.

Their servant was dead.

I was their killer.

Chapter 2

For a few minutes the only sound was of the fire, crackling and spitting and hissing, marked by the rhythmic click and clack of Hank opening and closing his Zippo.

"Tell me something from earlier on," Nick said after watching the fire's reflection dancing in Hank's eyes. It was the only trace of life in Hank's face as the rest of his features were like stone. "Maybe one of the first few times you changed. Or of the night you were cursed."

"Not ready yet for the latter, Nick," Hank said then took a sip from his cider. "But I'll tell you about the first night I changed."

Put You Down
Kelsey Town, Connecticut 1701

The full moon came a few days after I was cursed. I was out bringing the day's compost out to the pigs after supper. Those animals loved that treat at the end of the day.

My daughter was the only thing on my mind as I dumped the corn cobs, stale bread, bones and other kitchen slop out of the bucket into the pig pen. What happened at Chatfield Hollow the night my daughter went missing solved nothing. Gave us no new clues to where she was, brought me no closer to hugging her again.

After the townsfolk burned the witch's cabin to the ground, she was dead and wouldn't be telling us any of her secrets or confessing to taking my daughter.

And I had not been feeling right for a few days. I had broken a few tools while working. Breaking cast iron tools with my bare hands, seemed odd at the time but I wrote it off quickly because my mind was elsewhere.

I had been sleeping poorly as well. Nightmares of being caged, walking on all fours close to the ground, and an uneasiness of death around every corner.

My younger daughters were in the house with their mother cleaning up after dinner.

That was lucky for them.

As I finished dumping out the slop for the pigs I noticed something in the mud under the fence. I knelt down and yanked it out of the muck. It was a silk ribbon embroidered with the initials HK. My wife kept all of our daughters hair held back with ribbons like that one. This ribbon belonged to my oldest as those were her initials. It was the one embellishment we allowed our daughters to wear, and only while at our home. My wife preferred to keep their white caps as pristine as she could for church and that wasn't possible if they wore them around the farm.

I dropped the bucket, and held the ribbon with both hands, my knees in the mud and slop and muck soaking into my pants, chilling my skin.

The texture of the silk and the embroidered letters was marred by the mud and dirt. The original baby blue of the silk was completely lost to its time partially buried. I began to rub the ribbon between my fingers, desperate to feel the waxy smoothness of the fabric. But the grit from its haphazard grave made that impossible.

Jumping over the fence, I ran to the water trough in with the pigs and plunged my hands into the cold water. I scrubbed the ribbon, grinding it between the flesh of my finger tips and palms hoping to see a glimmer of the shimmering that the fabric once held.

But my tenacity was much stronger than the ribbon. Before I could register what I was doing, the fabric was not just torn aport, but rather obliterated as the water grew murky from the heat and muck and particles of silk turning to a grayish-black ash. The smell of burning silk is unmistakable, a mixture of charred meat and burned hair.

I pulled my hands out of the water, held them up in front of me as tears welled in my eyes.

My hands changed first.

Right before my eyes.

At first I thought it was merely the distorted view one gets seeing the world through tears.

My palms swelled and claws grew out of the ends of my fingers, tearing the flesh with how fast and violent they came. The pain brought me to my knees, then I crumpled to the hay covered ground. I curled up into a ball feeling like my insides were about to meet the world. First I threw up, then my bowels and my bladder let go.

I don't know how long I was unconscious. My eyes opened slowly. It was still dark out, but the moon was full casting shadows outside the barn door.

It was quiet around me. No rustling, or snorting or slopping noises like you hear in a pig barn. I was laying on the ground, in the hay and muck. I looked down to find myself naked, covered in mud and blood. My stomach was killing me, like I was over stuffed but had kept eating and eating and eating.

My nostrils were filled with the mixture of copper, dirt, and pig shit.

Pain shot through my gut, and out to every inch of my body. Like lightning trying to get out of me. I curled up again, praying for it to stop. Tears slammed against the back of my closed eyelids and the agony rocking through my spine was not natural.

Then it receded. So fast that my head spun. I rolled over and pushed my self up on my hands and knees. Lifted my head up to see twenty dead pigs torn apart all around the barn.

My brain was doing summersaults in my head and what felt like lightning shot through my stomach again. This time it brought everything up from my belly and I painted the walls with bile and raw pig meat. Pounds of it.

I fell back to the ground clutching at my sides.

I laid there for a few moments, then I heard my name. My wife was screaming for me from the back door of our home.

I didn't know what to do. I couldn't remember what I had done, but I knew I had killed my entire drift of young pigs. The older sows were in the other barn, but most of what I had was laying in pieces around me.

My wife's voice was louder, terror filled her call for me. She must have heard what had happened in the barn, but was smart enough to stay away until the noise had died down. From the blood and guts and flesh around me there must have been a chorus of pig screams accompanied by ripping and tearing noises like no one has heard before.

But I didn't know if it was going to happen again. I didn't know what had happened, but I was sure I wasn't going to let it happen around her or my daughters.

I scrambled to my feet, and ran for the woods. I felt odd and light on my feet. I only noticed a few miles in, how far I had gotten. I was at the edge of the deepest part of the brook in the middle of what is now Chatfield Hollow faster than I ever should have been able to get on foot.

I looked up at the sky praying as hard as I could but finding no answers or help.

Falling to my knees in the muck on the water's edge, I looked out over the glass-like water reflecting the moonlight. I crashed to my chest into the water and pulled myself in until I could swim freely. The water was cold, but I didn't care.

Swimming out to the center, I felt I had only one choice.

Sink.

I dove under the water and started swimming straight down. I opened my mouth and breathed in, deeply. My body fought the water, but I breathed in again, filling my lungs.

Then the pain rocked through my spine again.

I woke up in the tall grass about a quarter mile down stream where it got rocky as the sun was just peeking through the trees over the horizon.

I washed off the blood and the muck before I walked through the woods to my farm.

I didn't say anything to my wife when I walked in. I merely shook my head, went to the bedroom and laid down.

Chapter 3

"Is it a habit of pigs to eat like that?" Nick asked. "Or is that a side effect of the curse?"

"Six of one, half dozen of the other." Hank said. "Pigs are smart but they are also opportunistic omnivores. They will eat anything and everything in front of them."

"Interesting," Nick said.

"Why is that interesting?"

"I always figured pigs only ate certain foods," Nick said.

"They're basically garbage disposals," Hank said. "They often times literally eat garbage. And they will eat every last scrap in front of them if they like it."

"So what happened at your home here in Kelseytown and in Missouri was a mixture of your curse and typical behavior of a pig? Not one or the other?"

"Yeah."

"Okay, moving on then. What comes next?"

"Trying to remember events in order isn't easy," Hank said and tossed a new log onto the fire. Embers jumped up into the air and smoke drifted off the ash.

"You don't have to remember them in order," Nick said. "Just keep talking. I'll remember everything."

"Yeah, you and your little gift," Hank growled. "It's easier if you ask me questions."

"Well, did you know what you were after changing that first time?"

"Not exactly. We don't get a manual when we get cursed."

"It would help if you tell me about the night you were cursed, step by step. It would take care of a lot of the questions I have."

"You know very well how the curse works."

"Yes, I know how it works. But I only know like four bullet points from the night you were cursed. You told me and Mina that night at Chatfield Hollow when we met you and Gert that you 1) killed a witch, 2) back in 1701, 3) that we should run if we didn't want to be murdered by you and 4) that you were a monster not a man." Nick looked directly at Hank.

"I don't want to talk about that," Hank mumbled and flicked the Zippo open. "But I did learn a few small pieces that first year."

The Zippo snapped shut.

Dirt
Nantucket, Massachusetts 1702

Put it together right away that the full moon brings it on. Found excuses to go off into the wilderness away from my family and people during those days. After my six or seventh hunting trip, people started whispering about a monster roaming the hills. The hills that I had been hiding in during my episodes. Luckily, one of my father's investments in a Whaling Company had called me to my family home in Nantucket. The full moon was coming and I was left with little choice on how to deal with the situation. Luckily, my wife had stayed behind at the farm with our daughters. My brothers were also unable to make the trip because of other obligations. But I was still worried that I would hurt someone.

My gut instinct was to start swimming and just keep going. I knew from experience that my strength and my stamina were far beyond the limits of mortal men. Being stronger and faster and having extremely precise senses was a blessing, and it was easy to get lost in the potential of those gifts. But the very real possibility of hurting someone, especially someone you love, was always eating away at my conscience.

But even though I had tried to end my life once before and it didn't take, part of me was afraid as I swam out into the ocean, that if I went too far I wouldn't return.

The next morning, I woke up in bed.

I didn't know what bed.

I was bloated and covered in blood. The linens stuck to my skin where the blood had dried. My mind raced with what I could have done to be covered in blood. Did I kill a deer? Or a horse? Did I hurt someone? Kill someone? Those questions came fast, but I knew the answer from the smell of the blood before I got to the last one.

I got out of bed and looked out the window to see the familiar view of Nantucket from my family home.

Over the smell of the blood I noticed I wasn't alone in my house. A man was sitting in one of the chairs in my drawing room downstairs. He was very much alive, and I could smell he wasn't a normal man. He smelled of the sea, not like a fisherman, but like the fisherman's prey.

I panicked for a moment, not knowing if I should clean up and greet this man sitting in my home uninvited, or try and run. But running seemed out of the question.

Even though I could run fast, this man downstairs smelled like he could swim laps around me and we were on an island.

Through the window it was plain to see I had no where to go but downstairs.

So, I washed off what I could from my face and arms, and put on some clothes.

When I walked downstairs, the man sitting there looked directly at me and said, "Henry Kelsey, my name is Benjamin Pike."

"What are you doing in my house, Mr. Pike?" I asked

"The simple answer, Mr. Kelsey, is that I know what you are," Benjamin said. "It would be more comfortable if you sat down for what I have to say next."

I sat down in the chair across from him.

"I am also cursed," Benjamin said. "No use in beating around the bush."

"Cursed?" I raised an eyebrow.

"Yes, Mr. Kelsey, cursed. You and I did something to incur the wrath of a witch. Our mortal bodies, these vessels that our souls captain for our usually brief lives, were forced to house the spirit of an animal as well as our own soul. This duality causes a great deal of turmoil inside of creatures like us. For some of our days we can mostly control it, but during a full moon, you have found yourself lost in the animalistic nature of your forced passenger, haven't you?" Benjamin asked.

I nodded.

"And do you have gaps in your memories from those moments where your soul is losing the battle?" Benjamin asked.

"Bits and pieces," I said.

"I don't suppose you remember any bits or pieces from last night?" Benjamin asked.

"No," I shook my head and looked down at the floor.

"I can smell the blood, you're covered under your clothes," Ben said. "And either you're a pig farmer or your forced passenger is a very unlucky swine."

"Both actually," I said quietly.

"Interesting," Ben said and stood, "What do you remember from last evening?"

"Why are you so curious about what I was doing last night?" I asked, my teeth clenched together.

"I will show you why," Ben said. "if you will take a short walk for men like us."

I stood up and followed Ben outside. He started for the street, and with every step his pace quickened. I kept up easily until we were running faster than most eyes could follow.

A few minutes of running through the thick under brush, easily side stepping thicker trees and jumping over downed logs, Benjamin slowed to a normal walk as the forest opened up to a small shack.

Ben stopped outside the front door that was only hanging from the bottom hinge, askew in the doorway. I stopped next to him and smelled the air.

"This his blood I'm covered in?" I asked.

"Yes," Benjamin said. "His name was Samuel Bishop. He was a bit of a recluse, lived on his own on the far side of the island about as far from everyone else as he could be."

"I went out into the ocean last night to avoid something like this," I said and fell to my knees. "I should have swam further, hoping to never return to this world."

"You aren't always the one making the decisions even when you think you're in control, with our affliction. I spend my uncontrollable nights deep in the ocean," Ben said and knelt down beside me. "It has helped me from hurting anyone for many years."

"How long have you been like this?" I asked.

"Forty-one years," Benjamin said.

"What are we?" Hank asked.

"We are the cursed," Ben said. "Specifically, we are Weres. I know you've heard the old tales of men who changed into wolves during the full moon, just as I did growing up. Maybe even frightened a few children with the stories yourself. But did you never think that these might be more than interesting ways to pass a long dark evening?"

"But those stories are always about wolves," I said.

"Romanticizing the past, Mr. Kelsey," Ben said. "Werewolf sounds much more dramatic than Werelobster."

"Or Werepig," I said.

"I was thinking hog," Benjamin said.

"I haven't been castrated," I said. "Hogs are castrated adult males that you're getting ready for market. Helps them fatten up."

"Well, it doesn't just roll off the tongue like werewolf," Ben said.

"This man, Bishop, I didn't mean to hurt him," I said.

"I'm not here to take you in or convince you to turn yourself in Mr. Kelsey," Ben said. "No one will even notice him missing, not for a very long time at least. As I said, he is reclusive, and his remains will be seen as the result of a wild animal attack."

"What do I do now, then?" I asked.

"You follow your instincts, get as far from people as you can in the hopes that you can avoid hurting anyone," Ben said.

"I still don't understand why I am cursed," I said.

"Did you break the heart of a witch?" Ben asked.

"No, why would I be romantically involved with such a creature?" I said.

"They don't always come with warts and a broomstick," Ben said. "So, then you killed one."

I said nothing.

"That is much more common, in our uncommon predicament. She used her last moments and the last of her magic to force the animal's spirit into you. As you said, you are a pig farmer and I would guess your animals were close at hand. Just as in my case, a lobster was available," Ben smirked, but shook his head slightly letting the smile fall away. "Close at hand, so it goes."

"Is there a way to stop this?" I asked. "A cure?"

"Not that I have found, and the one witch I have ever been able to track down laughed at me," Ben said.

"How many cursed men have you found in your travels?" I asked.

"Only one other, but he had met a few around the world in his journeys," Ben said.

"How old were you when you were cursed?" I asked.

"I was forty-one years old," Ben said.

I thought about that for a moment, turning over those two numbers he had given me, before I spoke. "We don't suffer naturally as others, do we?"

"We do not. The other that I had met claimed to have been cursed over two hundred years ago," Ben said. "I do my best to keep to myself these days. I have little need to actually interact with the people of this island, or this world. This works well for me, but could drive another man insane from loneliness. But it is a life I highly suggest for the sake of any future Samuel Bishops that might cross your path other wise."

"I have a family, a wife and daughters. I want to have sons as well," I said.

"I don't think that's possible, but it is your life and your curse," Ben said and stood up. "I don't have any more to say than that."

"Can I find you if I have more questions?" I asked.

"You will have many more questions," Ben said. "But you can find me if you need to. I spend most of my time on or in the ocean. I dock off the southern part of the island when I am not avoiding people all together."

"I think I should give him a proper burial," I said.

"You may do as you wish, but I've long been done with burying my dead in the dirt," Benjamin stood up. "I hope you find a balance to our cursed life, Mr. Kelsey. God knows I am still searching."

I was looking at the ground as Ben disappeared.

I buried Samuel Bishop under a giant Oak close to his home in the woods with only the tree marking his grave.

Chapter 4

"I'm doing all this sharing. I hate talking about myself the whole time. You tell me something?" Hank said, then drained the last of his beer.

"I wish I could have asked Frank Stone if he remembered anything of his lives from before he was resurrected," Nick said.

Hank sat there, quiet, searching for something to say.

"I sentenced him to death without considering if he remembered the lives of the men who were used to create him," Nick said. "What were the names of their wives or their children? I was only a teenager and I had Mina execute him without asking him about who might have missed the people he was before he was created. It keeps me awake most nights."

"I forget that I don't like it when you share," Hank said and grabbed another beer from the cooler.

"Let's focus on you then," Nick said. "I'm curious if your wife ever found out what you are?"

"She did," Hank said quietly.

Shame In You
Kelsey Town, Connecticut - 1711

The two daughters I still had grew up as they tend to do. The older of them, Abigail, had gotten married at sixteen which was typical of the time. But our youngest, Elizabeth, was still living with my wife and I into her late teens. She did not conform to the standards of the time. She was adventurous, disappearing for days at a time until I tracked her down when

I had enough of her games.

I found her in the arms of a married man. A well respected man in our town. My first instinct was to tear him to pieces. Broke his arm instead and he never fully gained the use of it after.

The part about him being well respected was a problem for me and my family though. He was a town Selectman, and a merchant. And an accusation like mine would fall on deaf ears. A man of his stature would never admit or be held accountable for such a sin.

And soon after that altercation, we discovered the other problem. My daughter was pregnant from their affair.

My wife and I did the only thing we could think to do. Elizabeth and my wife moved to our home on Nantucket, where my wife thoroughly convinced the world that she was pregnant with my child. I would visit as often as I could, but I was here when my first grandchild was born, Charles Henry Kelsey.

My wife and I had been trying for a long time to have another child, I had no sons to carry on my name. But now, there was a child to carry on the Kelsey name.

I had a grandson to raise.

But fate proposed a different path.

The first few months were especially difficult. My daughter's health declined as she nursed the boy, and his suffered as well. Her behavior was erratic, verging on manic. One day she would be ecstatic, loving, happy and playful with the child and her mother and I. The next she would be sullen and withdrawn. She wouldn't feed the child on these days. The withdrawal began to take over more and more days in a row.

She would ignore the child's cries for attention. My wife and I tried everything we could to make her do her duty.

"The boy will starve if you do not feed him, Beth," my wife pleaded with my daughter.

"You feed him! To the world you're his mother, why not now too," Beth said.

"Because it does not work like that," my wife said. "Don't be a foolish child and make this boy suffer more than he has to because of your actions."

"Oh, he's suffering because of my actions now is he?" Beth yelled.

I wanted to scream at my daughter, to put her in her place. To point out her faults and shame her. But I was dealing with my own demons.

The full moon was coming.

In the beginning, the cursed are stronger and faster. But as we change and in our other form, we are even stronger. And I felt it fill my veins.

It was only half past five and sunset wasn't for another hour. My plan was to be as far from everyone out in the ocean as I could get by that time. But it seems this curse had more surprises for me.

Beth became violent towards my wife, shoving her to the floor. My daughter reached for the boy, but I grabbed her arms stopping her in her tracks.

Beth struggled, and screamed, but it was little use compared to my strength.

My wife saw my hands change.

The look of terror in her eyes was unmistakable.

My wife screamed, "What kind of devil work was that, Henry?" She pushed herself to her feet and pulled our daughter away from me. I let her go gently, putting my hands behind my back.

I had nothing to say. I had tried everything I could not to drag her into what I had become. But when she saw what looked like clawed monster's hands attached to me, holding our daughter, my wife started making connections she didn't understand, yet knew were bad. All those times I was away, during the full moon. The fact that she was looking much more our age than I was. And we had tried for so many years to have more children after having our first three with no real obstacles or worries.

"Leave now, Henry," My wife said quietly and coldly. "You do not belong here any longer."

Beth was now weeping softly into the crook of my wife's arm.

I stood there for a moment knowing she was right.

I sold off all of my pigs, using the excuse of new business ventures to explain why I was going to be spending most of my time away from my farm. And people believed that my wife was raising my son on Nantucket. Fortunately, my other business ventures had become very fruitful and my wife, daughter and grandson never wanted for anything. But I kept my distance. Ben helped me a great deal through those years, as he was accustom to hiding on that island, watching his children go on to have families of their own.

Years went by far too quickly. My grandson grew to be a man, my daughter evened out becoming an excellent mother, and age took hold of my wife.

In her last moments, she asked for me. I was close by listening. When I walked into our bedroom, I had not been in there for twenty-two years.

"Hello Henry," my wife said hoarsely through a smile.

"Hello my love," I said.

My daughter looked at me trying to understand, "Father. How is this possible? You look exactly like you did on the day you left."

"Magic, sadly," my wife said.

"What does that mean, mother?" Beth said. My wife did not answer her, nor did I.

"Henry, can you show me what you really are? Does it work that way?" My wife asked.

"Yes, I can show you," I said. "You must leave us alone for a moment, Beth. Do not come back in here until I tell you to."

"I will do no such thing," Beth said.

"Beth," my wife said quietly. "Please give us a moment."

With an exasperated sigh, Beth left the room.

"It is remarkable Henry," my wife said. "You haven't aged a single day in thirty years."

"Remarkable, yes, but all I can recall is pain," I said. "These years not being by your side, with our family."

"You've always been close by though, haven't you?" she asked.

"Yes, and I will continue to watch over our children and grand children as long as I live."

"Show me, Henry," my wife said. "I'm not afraid anymore."

I stood there for a moment searching her eyes. Not sure what I expected to see in them, but what I found was curiosity like I had seen in the first days of our courtship.

I began undressing and looked away from her to the floor. I only met her gaze when I was finished.

"Show me, Henry," she said. "Oh, I've missed saying your name."

I nodded, raised one hand and let it change. I kept my attention on her eyes. I had missed those eyes on me. The way she saw through all that was in the way of who I truly was, all the pain and the barriers I was taught to put up, to survive as a man in the society at the time, and then what I learned to survive as a monster.

She saw through all of that.

The change was always painful, but this time it was excruciating. The clock seemed to stop as my hands enlarged, bones cracking as my fingers stretched, the flesh strained and tore from the stress. The sound of my nails thickening and growing from the ends of my fingers like sharpened hooves from each finger was sickening.

Her eyes widened. Then I showed her my other hand.

My wife looked into my eyes and nodded gently.

I closed my eyes so I would not see her face, to focus my control and let the change happen. It had taken decades to learn how to keep control of my mind during those times I chose to change, compared to the times the moon takes me, but I knew I wouldn't hurt her.

To this day I have no idea what someone sees when I change completely. I have never been able to bring myself to look in a mirror on purpose as it happens, but I know that it must be horrific from the way it feels; bones cracking, flesh tearing and stretching and healing as the pig showed its face. And the tusks, those are the most painful part, growing and pushing my teeth out of the way, ripping through my gums and breaking my jaw only to heal back together in less than a heartbeat.

"Open your eyes Henry," she said.

I obeyed, and found my wife looking directly into my soul the way only she ever could. She had to strain to look up at me as my head touched the ceiling in that form.

"You can still understand me like this, Henry?" she asked.

I nodded.

"Can you speak?"

I shook my head slowly.

"You're much too tall like this." She choked on a laugh.

I don't know what it looked like to her but I smiled and held back a chuckle, not knowing if it would have come out as a grunt or a growl or something even more horrifying.

"Please change back, Henry."

I changed and reached for my pants.

"I wish things could have been different, Henry."

As I pulled on my shirt I said, "As do I, my love. But this is the hand we were dealt."

"I don't think I will be here much longer," my wife said. "You know that, though, don't you?"

"I'm going to get Beth," I said. "I will be right back. As long as that is all right?"

My wife smiled and nodded gently.

I walked into the hallway, and Beth was over near the window that looked out over the water.

"Beth, your mother only has a little more time with us," I said.

"How do you know? She's been like this for a week," Beth said, not looking at me.

"I just know, Beth," I said. "I am going to stay here with you and your mother tonight. She wants me to be here."

Beth turned, looked at me, and walked back into my wife's bedroom.

Not much was said over the next few hours, as my wife grew weaker and weaker. Beth sat on my wife's left side and I sat on her right. I took her hand as she slipped away, listening to her heart beat for the last time.

Chapter 5

Nick sat there staring into the fire. He opened his mouth, about to say something, but Hank mumbled, "I don't want to talk about that yet."

The fingers of Hank's left hand flicked the Zippo open, then his large hand wrapped around the brass case closing it with a muffled clank.

"You're gonna have to at some point."

"Do I?" Hank said still clutching the lighter in his hand.

"You've always been a real charmer haven't you," Nick said.

"Coming from the guy that visits me on a weekly if not daily basis," Hank said.

"Touché," Nick said. He reached over to the pile of logs, grabbed one and dropped it on the fire. Sparks crackled into the air. "Now onto the next story."

"I can't think of anything," Hank said.

"Bullshit, I can see the gears turning behind your eyes," Nick said.

"Give me one of your ridiculous prompts," Hank said.

"Fine, tell me about your biggest regret?" Nick asked.

"Nice try," Hank said.

"Then tell me about your second biggest regret," Nick said.

"A few years ago, I was at Chatfield Hollow and warned a couple of teenagers to run rather than just kill them when I was learning some new curse management skills," Hank said.

"Funny," Nick said and faked a smile. "This is supposed to be a conversation about stories of yours I don't know. And for the record having been one of those teenagers that was the single scariest moment of my life."

"Do you actually know my side of it?" Hank asked.

"I know enough," Nick said. "And I've talked and written about that time of our lives more than enough."

"The only thing I can think of then would be the last time I went to Vegas," Hank said. "When Mina and I went to the Great Comet Tournament."

"What now?" Nick sat straight up.

"Oh," Hank said. "Did your wife forget to mention to you that we went to the tournament after The Great Comet Hukata?"

"Do you mean Comet Hyakutake?" Nick said. "Are you fucking with me?"

"Not at all," Hank said. "Seems you may not know as much as you think you do."

I Know Somethin' ('bout you)
Las Vegas, Nevada - 1996

Mina told me she was calling in one of the many favors I owed her. She was standing at the stove making marinara sauce from scratch. It had fresh mushrooms in it. She was doing that on purpose. The two of you had moved into Gertrude's house right after your wedding, finally putting it to use after ten years of her being gone.

"How many favors do you think I owe you?" I asked sitting at the table with a pint glass of beer in front of me.

"How many years have you known me?" Mina asked then dipped her finger into the sauce and tasted it.

"About ten," I said.

"3700," she said with a cold, straight face as she dashed more pepper into the pan.

"Is that one for roughly every day I've known you?" I asked. "That's fucked up."

"Yup," she said. "And you know what is happening next month."

"Yes," I said. "But you must be joking."

"Nope," Mina said. "And you're going with me."

"Why don't you bring Nicholas?" I said. "You two do everything together."

"Not this," she said. "He doesn't understand the tournament, not yet."

"I don't want to go," I said.

"That's why I'm calling in a favor," Mina said.

"And making some of my favorite food?" I said.

"I'm not a savage Hank," she said.

"Keep telling yourself that, Amazon," I said. "Why can't you go yourself?"

"I'm powerful, Hank, not stupid," she said. "Believe it or not I'll stick out way more by myself."

"That leaves a little problem though," I said and took a sip of beer. "You're weakling for a husband, Nicholas."

"No problem at all, Penny is capable enough to watch his back for a few days," Mina said. "She's still not showing any sign of sticking with only one form."

"Other than the sparrow, I don't think I've seen her change into the same thing twice," I said. "I think she is just like the shapeshifter legends we have heard."

"Exactly," Mina said as she strained the ziti in the sink. "So, I'm not worried. Nick will be fine with her around for a few days."

"I'm pretty sure he will also know the tournament is happening," I said. "Not much gets past him and that stupid ability of his."

"True but he has a bunch of stuff going on with the renovations they're doing at the Stanton House," Mina said. "And I will tell him we are going antiquing up in Maine and he won't suspect anything."

"He loves antiquing though," I said. "Won't he be jealous and wonder why we are doing it without him?"

"Yeah, but he has to be around while they work on the house. His mother and grandmother are off on their road trip to Panama in their RV. He'll be focused on us doing something he loves without him, get all pissy because he can't get away and when he gets all pissy he tends to clam up about his feelings."

"A Red Herring more or less," I said.

"Exactly."

"I'll go with you but I'm not sure I can lie so he'll believe it."

"All you have to do is keep your mouth shut and let me do the talking if he asks any questions," Mina said.

"How are we going to get there?" I asked.

"We're going to fly in a big metal bird called a plane through the air defying gravity and then have a controlled crash called a landing," Mina said.

"I meant do you want to drive, fly or run there, asshole," I said.

"I'm not running all that way or sitting in a car with you're intolerable ass for three days," Mina said.

"Forty-nine hours," I said.

"What?" Mina asked.

"I can do that drive in forty-nine hours," I said.

"I would rather be water boarded for forty-nine hours than sit in a car with you for that amount of time," Mina said. "Flights on me."

"Fine," I said. "You're loss."

"How is spending only six hours on the same plane in different rows than you a loss over sitting in the same car with you for forty-nine hours?" Mina asked.

"Roadside attractions," I said.

"I live in a world where ghosts, were pigs, vampires, werewolves, leprechauns, werellamas and zombies exist and you think I give a shit about the worlds largest ball of twine?" Mina asked.

"I meant a little more along the lines of the ghosts, vampires, werecreatures, leprechauns and zombies than extra large balls," I said. "And if i'm not mistaken you and I don't need to sit in a car to travel with each other along the open road."

"You gonna finally buy a bike?" Mina asked.

"Finally in your time with me but I've had more bikes than you," I said. "Last bike I owned was an Indian, but we can get whatever you prefer. And I recommend we rent bikes for the trip, and I'll take care of it so there's a buffer between Nick and the rental."

"Are you seriously that afraid of flying?"

"I just don't want to bring about thousands of terrible scenarios because of a stupid idiom coming true," Hank said.

"That is the dumbest thing I have ever heard you baby," Mina said.

"Planes are terrible inventions and remove the adventure in travel," I said. "Makes the getting there much less earned."

"I was only thinking of being away for three or four days," Mina said as she shook the last bit of water off of the ziti in the sink.

"Wuss," I said.

"How is not wanting to spend that much time with you being a wuss?" Mina asked as she turned the stove off. "It might make for a great story when its all said and done but I just want to go out there for a few days and watch the tournament. And I can't go alone, not only for my own sake but also for the safety of every other creature that will be there."

"The whole point of the tournament is so that you and you're kind have a bit of 'Natural Selection' helping you keep the supernatural world in check. It's not for you to go and fulfill your bloodlust."

"Again, that is why I am asking you to go with me," Mina said.

"I can't physically stop you," I said.

"But I might listen to you," Mina said.

"Might?" Hank said. "Penny would be able to help you there better than I could."

"I can't ask her to go back there, not after everything we went through to get out of there back in '86. You know more than anyone how much she has had to work through after being forced to fight to the death in that tournament. It was nothing short of a miracle she is as well adjusted as she is. I don't think any other nine year old girl could go through that and still be a functioning member of society," Mina said. "But I do know from experience that you aren't as mentally fragile."

"Can we at least go up to Area 51 while we're out there?" I asked as she made up two plates of pasta at the counter.

"We can even rent bikes and ride up there," Mina said as she put the plate of pasta in front of me.

"Maybe you're not a total savage," I said as I picked up my fork and dug into the pasta.

*****

Mina told you that she was meeting me in Nantucket, but I actually left five days before her and took that cross country trip on a Harley like she and I discussed. I slept under the stars every night and it was fantastic. I've wanted to rub it in her face for a long time but always kept it to myself because I didn't want you to accidentally hear us talking about it.

I'll have to tell you that story because it was a good one.

Vegas was very different from what I remember.

And not in a good way.

I had booked us rooms in Caesar's Palace as The Sands had been demolished and Caeser's was across the street from Bally's, where the tournament was being held. Wanted to be close, but not in the same building as everything that as going on. Plus, I like the whole Roman Empire theme.

After checking in and cleaning up, I walked down and met Mina at the airport on the southern end of The Strip.

Luckily she packs light and only had a backpack with her so we just walked back to the hotel. We headed west on Tropicana back to the Strip rather than heading up Paradise to Flamingo. We covered that distance quickly as there weren't many people, but when we got to The Strip we blended into the crowds there.

"This place is a little different than I remember it," Mina said as they walked. "And thank God its not as hot."

"A bit," I said.

"Not like these are historical buildings that need to be preserved or something," Mina said.

"Guess not," I said.

"I'm getting hungry," Mina said. "The food on the plane wasn't exactly enough."

"Caesar's has one of the best buffets in Vegas," I said.

"That's the real reason you booked the rooms there, isn't it?" Mina asked.

"Yes," I said.

"Have you seen anyone from our part of the world?" Mina asked.

"A few," I said. "But I didn't go into Bally's."

"I'm a little nervous about walking in there myself," Mina said. "I almost brought the place down on my own head last time I was in there."

"So I've heard," I said.

"What did you hear about that day?" Mina asked.

"You were there," I said. "What could I tell you that you don't know."

"For starters, I was trying to save Penny's life and didn't have any idea what my actions would amount to, so I was a little distracted," Mina said.

"You were unaware of the implications of your actions? You don't say?" I said.

"Fuck you," Mina said. "Let's get a little more specific to our current situation. What are people whispering about coming into this tournament?"

"Some are wondering if the old magic still holds," I said. "They still feel compelled to be here, the draw is still present, but there is a fear that what you did, breaking the most powerful of the spells binding this whole thing together, has changed it."

"From everything that I have learned what I did should not affect this tournament," Mina said. "I wasn't ever held to the same spells."

"I know that's the real reason you wanted to be here," I said. "To see if you broke the whole thing."

"On only a few, very poorly documented occasions, has my kind ever participated in the tournament and it kept going as it was intended when the next Great Comet came by," Mina said.

On the sidewalk there was a street vender selling sunglasses and Mina stopped and picked out the biggest pair she could find, handed the guy 5 bucks for them.

"Maybe we should just find you a full mask of some sort," I said.

"I think that would attract a lot more attention than a young woman wearing fashionably large sunglasses and a hoodie," Mina said and flipped the hood of her sweatshirt up covering even more of her head and face.

"No one would question either in this town," I said as we walked into the entrance of Caeser's.

"Lead on to the buffet," Mina said. "I'm starting to hate you a little too much and I'm gonna blame it on hunger rather than your personality for now."

So, we went and ate.

I think the staff hated us by the time we left.

*****

After we dropped Mina's bag off in her room we walked over to Bally's.

With every step closer to the main entrance, I was expecting the place to implode or for flames to sprout up the side of the building. But as we walked through the door, nothing.

People hustled past us in and out of the doors and nothing shook.

"That was anticlimactic," Mina said.

I looked at her and shook my head in annoyance.

"Now let's see if we can get into the arena," Mina said.

Since magic was involved and no one wants frail humans to be wandering into the arena, the entrance is through a set of security doors near the back of the casino floor. Hidden in plain sight, with a simple spell that makes anything that doesn't have a supernatural bent feel horribly uncomfortable.

Mina and I walked through the doors, and started down the stairs.

The first two flights were quiet but at the third I could feel a hum through the steps. On the fourth flight the hum turned to a dull roar and got loader with every step down until we hit the bottom of the fifth flight where I could feel and hear the roar all at once.

I looked at the doors leading into the top of the stands, then to Mina.

"Ready?" Mina asked.

I nodded as Mina pushed the doors open.

The energy smacked you in the face, as there was a fight in progress and the crowd was on their feet screaming, jeering, rooting and ready to explode.

"Holy shit, the Minotaur," Mina said. "Who is he fighting? I don't see anyone else."

The Minotaur was looking up and we followed his gaze to find a giant snake falling toward the arena floor.

The Minotaur stomped one of his hooves into the dirt kicking up dust. He crouched down in the cloud and whipped his head around as the giant snake writhed in the air right above him. One of the Minotaurs horns came up through the jaw and out the top of the head of the snake. The Minotaur brought one of his giant hands down on the back of the snake's neck and yanked away from the serpent at the same time.

The horn that was sticking through the snake's head tore out the front of the creature's face and it fell limp on the arena floor.

The area fell silent, everyone seeming to hold their breath.

The Minotaur stood, soaked in blood, and cleared out his nose with a snort sending a cloud of red snot into the air around him. He reached down, picked up the limp serpent. He dug has thumbs into the gash his horn made in the snake's face and got a good grip on the two sides of its head. With another snort of bloody snot, the Minotaur tore the serpent in half long ways and roared.

The crowd erupted.

"Basilisk," I said.

"I wouldn't have figured a Basilisk to be a glory hound," Mina said.

"Could have been young and dumb, or a slave, who knows," I said. "Doesn't matter now."

"I want to talk to him," Mina said.

"Kind of impossible unless you have a time machine," I said.

"The Minotaur, jackass," Mina said.

The Minotaur walked to one of the arched doorways that lead into and out of the arena floor disappearing into the darkness.

"Lead the way then," I said.

"I'm trying to remember how the hell to get down to the locker rooms," Mina said.

"You could try running down and jumping into the arena and following him?" I said.

"That would be the opposite of keeping a low profile," Mina said and started walking toward another set of doors to the right of where we came in. On the other side was another set off stairs leading down.

We headed down again but took it at a much faster pace. At the bottom there were beings and creatures of all kinds moving through the main corridor of the labyrinth beneath the arena. Vampires made side bets with Leprechauns while Werecreatures traded stories of the weirdest places they've woken up and so many others that were making backroom deals or just catching up after years of not crossing paths.

I looked over the crowd but there were so many moving bodies readying for the next fight, placing bets and just plain in the way I couldn't make heads or tails of where to head next.

Mina stood still, closed her eyes and I could see her searching with her other senses.

I don't know how she could do it with that much distraction, but after a little over a minute she said, "Follow close behind."

She stepped into the throng, but as she walked everyone seemed to step away from her without even giving her a look. I followed closely in her wake as the space filled with bodies as we moved through.

At the end of the corridor we took a right into a room where the Minotaur was laying back on a table. A giant troll was bent over him, the Minotaur groaned in pain as we walked in.

Reaching up under her hoodie, Mina pulled a knife from the sheath hanging from her neck. As she brought it grew to its full length revealing a claymore that stood taller than she did. The magic of the swords transformation had worn off on me after seeing this trick so many times, but Mina's control and poise holding the giant blade is always unnerving.

The troll and the Minotaur both looked over at us. I had my arms folded as Mina pushed the hoodie off her head with her left hand.

The troll looked horrified and stepped away from the Minotaur.

"Do you always barge into a room brandishing that thing, Mina?" The Minotaur asked. "Put that down, you're scaring Larry."

"Larry?" Mina said lowering her sword. "And it's a habit of survival."

The sword shrank in Mina's hand to the size of a small knife and she slid it back into the sheath hanging around her neck. She tucked it back under hoodie.

"A bad habit when meeting new people," I said.

Mina stuck out her hand to the troll, and the monster shook it. "I'm Mina Dan this is Hank."

"Hi, I'm his massage therapist," Larry said, his hand trembling in hers.

I kept my arms folded.

"I think it's more to do with you thinking I won't recognize you without the sword but I'd recognize those eyes anywhere," the Minotaur said. "You still look like that little girl I met what seems like yesterday for me, Mina."

"That was a long time ago for me," Mina said. "Basically another lifetime."

"Me too, technically," the Minotaur said. "To what do I owe the pleasure of your company?"

"I... I saw the end of your fight and wanted to say hello," Mina said.

"You thought you broke the tournament didn't you?" The Minotaur asked.

"Bingo," I said. I really wished at that very moment that I had a toothpick or at least a stick of gum to chew. I could just tell I was about to be really bored.

Mina back handed me on the shoulder, but luckily I was standing firm and she didn't hit me that hard, so I only slide back a few inches. It was kinda of perfect because I was able to lean back against the wall next to the door.

"Maybe I should come back a little later and let you folks chat," Larry said as he slinked toward the door as much as a giant troll could slink.

"Yeah, this Charlie horse is still acting up," The Minotaur said. "I can still benefit from some more time with those gifted hands of yours, Larry."

"Nice to meet both of you," Larry said as he squeezed through the door backward closing it quietly behind him.

Of course it was awkwardly still after Larry left the room.

"You didn't break the tournament Mina," The Minotaur said.

"How do you know?" Mina asked.

"I've been to every single one and this one is just as normal and chaotic as every other tournament has ever been," he said.

"As chaotic as the last one?" Mina asked.

"In a different way," he said. "The magic is still binding those who enter it, to the death, as it did before you came in like a wrecking ball during the Halley's Comet tournament."

"Wait," I said, "You've been to every tournament? How old are you?"

"I've been around longer than I can recall," The Minotaur said.

"What is your actual name?" I asked. "I'm sick of referring to you as The Minotaur in conversation with her or in my own head. And is there jus the one of you or a bunch of Minotaurs running around somewhere?"

"Asterion," Mina said.

"Ah, you know your Greek Mythology, Mina," Asterion said. "And Hank, I am the only one."

"Are you really the child of a woman and a bull?" I asked. And I hoped that image of a bull fucking a woman is burned into your memory and that is haunts your nightmares for the rest of your days, Nicholas.

"Yes and no," Asterion said. "I am the result of powerful and vengeful creatures that didn't really understand their own magic getting angry at the other creatures that had evolved in their world and were beginning to take over."

"Gods," I said. I'm not sure if my eyes narrowed at the idea, but I certainly have an over whelming feeling that I looked skeptical at best.

"Powerful creatures," Asterion said. "I do not believe they were gods anymore than you or I are gods because of our long lives or that Mina is a god because she is super strong and nearly invincible. Nor that her ancestors were gods because they destroyed those that created me."

"Pardon me?" Mina said. "What did you just say?"

"You're ancestors the Amazons and the Tellers hunted down the old, powerful creatures and destroyed them. Just as Theseus went into the Labyrinth so he could destroy me to protect his people."

"But we keep the balance, we only kill when the supernatural world encroaches on the human world," Mina said. "Or vice versa."

"We are all natural, we all exist here," Asterion said. "But I understand that your first instinct was and still is to protect the weaker ones. It is in your nature. That is why I helped your kind create this tournament."

"You've known others like me?" Mina said.

"Many," Asterion said. "At some point in almost every single one of your predecessors lives, they seek me out."

"Why?" I asked. "Because you helped create this tournament?"

"That is part of it," Asterion said. "Do you know who created the Labyrinth, my home?"

"Daedalus," Mina said. "And I thought it was your prison."

"Synonymous in this case," Asterion said. "Daedalus did not create the Labyrinth of his own free will. When he was ordered to by King Minos, Daedalus's son was held prisoner so he would complete the task. But, Daedalus had been present during my conception, birth and early years. He helped my mother initially because she was his queen, but he recognized the love my mother had for me being similar to his love for his own son. This tore him apart as he knew my nature was not my own doing and she asked him to help me. So he built the Labyrinth so no one could find me. So that I could forever hide there as Daedalus hypothesized that I would resurrect if I were to be killed in the traditional sense."

"Why would he think that?" I asked.

"When they finally tried to sacrifice the bull that was my father, they could not," Asterion said.

"Wait, what about the human sacrifices of seven boys and seven girls every nine years or whatever it was?" I asked. "Is that true as well?"

"I much prefer venison," Asterion said. "But I didn't have much of a choice. King Minos ordered that to keep people subservient. I was trapped in there and aside from rats or other rodents, those children were the only food I was offered."

"Tell me more about these old powerful creatures her kind hunted down?" I asked.

"I don't know very much as they were destroyed before I was old enough to really understand how I was even created," Asterion said. "Your kind, Mina, did not take kindly to how they used my mother and many other women in their games. Their ploys for reverence. And the warrior who I met first took what happened to her nephew because of my creation, which resulted in irrational fear and control issues from the king, very personally."

"Who was her nephew?" I asked. I don't even know why I asked that thinking back, I didn't really care.

"Icarus," Mina whispered.

"Have you ever wondered where that sword of yours actually came from, Mina?" Asterion asked.

"My husband Nick's and my ancestors created it," Mina said.

"Dyna and her teller had a little bit of help from her brother," Asterion said. "Maybe more than a little."

"You remember her name?" Mina asked.

"I remember all of their names," he said and looked away as though he could look over his shoulder into the past. "I remember all of them."

"I...could..." Mina said struggling on how to ask all the questions she had at once.

"You may not have broken the tournament on your last visit but you broke your brain on this trip," I said and chuckled to myself.

Asterion and Mina looked at me and shook their heads.

Asterion focused his attention back on Mina, "I want to tell you everything Mina, but you need to understand that I have done this so many times now."

"We can meet again, later, if you need to rest," Mina said.

"It would be best to tell these stories somewhere other than here,"

Asterion said. "This tournament isn't quite the right place for those tales."

"You're right, its not what this is for," Mina said.

"Why did you guys create the tournament anyway?" I asked.

"So our kind, Hank, have a place to truly be what we are," Asterion said.

"What exactly is that?" I asked.

"Chaos," Mina whispered and Asterion nodded.

"Cute," I said.

"Will you answer one question now, Asterion?" Mina asked.

He nodded, "If I can."

"Why do you come to the tournament every time?" Mina asked.

"Creating the opportunity to meet you," Asterion said. "Lets meet later for a bit more privacy so we can get started on the tale of the women who came before you."

"We're staying over at Caesar's," Mina said.

"He can't exactly come over there and ring for us at the concierge, Mina," I said.

"Oh, right," Mina said.

"I'll meet you at midnight at the Ice Box Canyon Trail in the Red Rock National Park just outside the city."

"Sounds like a plan," Mina said.

I went with Mina but I honestly didn't pay attention to anything they talked about except for one fact. Daedalus is still alive - plays the guitar in that band the Rolling Stones. You'll have to ask her about all the rest.

Killer Is Me

Chapter 6

"Any other secrets you and Mina have been keeping from me you want to unload?" Nick asked.

"No," Hank said.

"You're going to have to just open up because I'm super annoyed and can't come up with any prompts," Nick said.

"Oh is your annoyingly know-it-all ass hurt that people were able to keep something from you?" Hank asked. "You're whole existence is predicated on keeping information hidden in plain sight."

"That wasn't hidden in plain site, it was kept from me," Nick said.

"It was right there the whole time, you just never asked the right questions," Hank said. "You can't know everything about everyone. Its not realistic or even possible."

"I can still be annoyed something was kept from me," Nick said. "Just go into another story so I can stew for the appropriate amount of time and let it go."

"You're not going to let it go," Hank said.

"Whatever happened to your daughters that survived and your grandchildren then?" Nick said through gritted teeth.

"Lots of stuff," Hank said.

"Like?" Nick said.

"That is a really broad question," Hank said. "My Beth had no more children and died on Nantucket. Her son, Charles Kelsey, he went onto have three children of his own that made it to adulthood, a son and two daughters. There came many more after that. Abigail had four daughters.

One of my descendants from her line is still living in Kelsey Town."

"Who?" Nick asked.

"Paul Stephenson," Hank said.

"Seriously?" Nick asked. "How did I never know you were related to him?"

"I never told you," Hank said.

"Thanks Captain Obvious," Nick said. "Why did you never mention that he is a descendent of yours?"

"Why would I have?" Hank said.

"Because that's kind of a big piece of information," Nick said and grabbed a beer from the cooler.

"No its not," Hank said.

"Seriously, the Kelsey Town Police Officer who has looked the other way or outright helped us on multiple occasions is your descendent? And it's not important. Does he know you're, you're…"

"His umpteen great grand daddy?"

"More along the lines of knowing you're playing the part of a distant cousin?"

"I have no idea if his family has kept up their family tree. I don't go to the family reunions or exchange Christmas cards."

"But you keep up with the family tree?"

"Of course I do."

"Interesting."

"Actually, its ridiculously boring."

"Why do it then?"

"Mostly because of routine with a bit of curiosity mixed in."

"Do you wish you could have some type of familial relationship with them?"

"That wouldn't be in my best interest. Isn't there something less tedious you want to ask me about?"

"Whatever," Nick said. "You told me a long time ago that you've fought in human wars. Want to tell me about that?"

"I've been to a few," Hank said. "But I don't mind starting with the first one."

Down In A Hole
Lexington & Concord 1775

It was April 19th, 1775. It was my 101st birthday and tension was at a breaking point between Great Britain and the Colonies. I had been helping smuggle arms and ammunition for the Minutemen. They had gotten a hold of plans from the British to search the area and seize the weapons. But the Continentals had their own plan. We scattered the weapons and readied for the invasion. A small engagement force of about a hundred met the British in Lexington, giving the British a sense of accomplishment, as the larger Imperial force scattered the minutemen easily.

Falling back to Concord, the Minutemen joined their main force of four hundred men. When the British broke into regiments to search the area for the weapons, that's when we hit them.

I had learned a great deal about the creature I had become by this point. It was a few days past the full moon, I had been hiding in the woods near what is now called Walden Pond, watching the movements of the scouts and spies from both sides as they but I still didn't know if joining this fight directly would be a good thing with this curse. My plan was to give a few men the idea to hide in the woods using the trees and brush as cover and help the Colonists smuggle munitions to key points. And they could spread the idea. This worked better than I could have ever imagined.

The typical style of combat in that era was simple and stupid. Two groups of men stood across from each other in an open field. They pointed their weapons across the field and fired. The British had more men and more guns. This usually left their enemy with only a few men standing and easy to subdue.

The main force of the British Regulars marched into Concord as three of their Companies broke off to search the area for the Colonial Militia's supplies. That's when we implemented our new tactics and came at the Red Coats from the forest, using the trees as cover. Our modest force of four hundred Militia men from across Massachusetts felt like three times that to the British. They had to regroup and were forced to utilize their only choice, a tactical retreat.

I felt more alive than I had in decades. Possibly ever.

We had scared them, we were something they had never seen. We kept hitting them from the cover of the forest, scaring them more and more.

This gave us two specific advantages.

As the Regulars marched toward Boston, the main force had sent out riders for all of their other companies to join them to give them a better chance of making it back onto the peninsula that used to be Boston.

This simply gave us more targets.

As the day wained, we had the bulk of the British forces in

Massachusetts retreating to Boston and Charlestown. By nightfall we had our blockade of the Boston Neck and the Charlestown Neck in place.

We now had the upper hand. The British were afraid and they were trapped. Boston looked much different back then. Boston was a peninsular city with the Charles River to the West and North and Boston Harbor to the East. Charlestown, now a part of Boston, was its own city to the North of the Charles River. Bunker Hill is in Charleston, but that comes up later in the Siege of Boston.

Both cities had very narrow necks of land connecting them to the rest of the colonies. This gave is the advantage of forcing them to fight with only one route for supply - the harbor. The channel between Charleston and Boston was easy for the British to get across, and they easily brought in supplies from Nova Scotia.

The first month saw small skirmishes, but meat was getting scarce, even with supplies coming in from the British Navel Fleet. And their horses were beginning to starve. This forced the British to abandon Charleston, easily consolidating their forces in Boston, fortifying key points to defend the city. Then they sent out scouting parties looking for livestock and hay on the islands around the harbor.

Our forces had grown even more with Colonies as far south as Maryland sending Militia Men to join our ranks. We had the man power now to confiscate the livestock and burned whatever we couldn't take with us like crops, barns full of hay, textiles and anything else we thought might be useful to the British.

The swell in our ranks from so many of the colonies gave cause to call us more than Minutemen or a Militia or rebels. It would be another month before it was made official, but we were a Continental Army, made up of men from across the colonies, and we were taking on the greatest Military force in the world, and we weren't losing.

This new army gave us a swell of hope and solidified that what we were doing was right. I felt justified in using my abilities to help these Colonists, to make a country of our own. And the extra hands brought new ideas to our fight. During this time Benedict Arnold, that traitorous piece of filth, and Ethan Allan were given the go ahead to raid Fort Ticonderoga where they secured more munitions and our first Navel Vessel.

I had stayed in Massachusetts to help with the Siege of Boston.

The full moon came on one of our raids. Four of us made our way to a suspected store house of grain that the British were hoping to empty on one of the Islands in Boston Harbor. The plan was to get in, burn it to the ground and leave before the scouts even arrived. We had spies everywhere in Boston and it was easy to get information out. The British were flying blind because they had no one on the outside to inform them of the Colonial Armies movements.

But the British had arrived earlier than planned and were well guarded and dug in like ticks when we arrived. We didn't see the cannon until it was too late. I only survived because of what I was.

Our kind heals quickly, but getting hit by cannon fire when you are in a row boat and try at the last second to save your fellow countrymen by taking the brunt of the hit isn't something you walk off. I awoke in the corner of a barn, my wrists and ankles bound with heavy iron shackles.

My eyes fluttered open and my body was on fire. Pain like I never imagined. I could feel my bones slowly mending, but very slowly. I couldn't focus, but I could see the three bodies of my friends around me. I couldn't hear their hearts. But I could hear the fifteen British Regulars heartbeats. Most were moving grain from the barn to their ship.

There were three soldiers looking over a map on a bale of hay with torches stuck into the ground around them. When one of them noticed me stirring, they all looked over to me. The Officer, I couldn't tell what he was and never found out his name or rank, stepped over to me, knelt down and looked into my face.

"You just lost me a days pay," the Officer said. He turned and looked to the other soldiers, "Seems it is your lucky day, men."

The Officer stood up and looked around the room. When he spotted what he was looking for, a hook hanging from a beam above their heads, he turned to his men and said, "Help me get him up."

The soldiers did as they they were asked and a few moments later I was hanging from the shackles on my wrists with my toes brushing the dirt. Pain coursed through every inch of me.

"So," the Officer said, "Your fellow rebels are dead, as you can see. Figured you would have succumbed to your injuries hours ago, but here you are."

My vision was still blurry, but I knew night had fallen. And through the open doorway, pools of moonlight bathed the grasses as a light wind brought the familiar smells of the farm into the barn.

"Will you offer your name, even if just for posterity of this failure of your operation?" The Officer said.

"No," I said through broken and bloody teeth.

"Will you tell me how you knew we were going to be here?" The Officer asked.

"No," I said.

"Is there any information that you will volunteer?" The Officer asked.

"If you let me go now, you might survive the night," I said.

The officer laughed, and turned to his men, "He's very funny, isn't he?"

The other soldiers were laughing as well.

I was wrapping my fingers around the chains above my head as a familiar pain joined my already taxed nerve endings. As usual, it was my hands that changed first. The shackles grew tighter as my hands and wrists swelled and morphed. The metal already giving way, creaking softly as my flesh expanded.

The officer, his attention still on his men, said, "I needed a good laugh after the past few months of dealing with you traitors."

When he turned his attention back to me he didn't see my hands, but he did see my other face. Terror replaced the grin in a flash as the Officer took in the face of his killer.

As in most cases, I didn't remember any of what had happened until hours after when I woke with the sun beginning to rise over the tree line on the East side of the island. I still don't remember everything. I know that in that moment, the soldiers screamed for the others, but the Officer's last word was traitor. Unless you consider the gurgling noises that came from the blood boiling up into his throat as I tore out his insides where he stood words.

The next day, I burned the bodies of the British Regulars along with the barn and the supplies.

I buried my friends under a Weeping Willow.

Chapter 7

"Have you ever met another Werepig?" Nick asked.

"I have not," Hank said. "And no one I have ever asked has heard of one either."

"So, you have searched out another like you?" Nick asked.

"I haven't gone hunting for one no, but once you begin meeting others who are afflicted with this curse, you learn what is out there," Hank said.

"Okay," Nick said. "I know you connected with Ben, the first Were creature you ever met—"

"First one I ever knew, but not the first one I ever met," Hank said.

"Please explain that?" Nick perked up.

"I found out many years later that one of my father's friends was cursed, his name was John O'Cuinn, an Irishman with a foul mouth," Hank said. "We had thought he had come to the Colonies as a Privateer through Salem, but it turns out he had actually been part of the first settlement at Roanoke."

"Why have you never introduced me to him?" Nick asked. "The answers I could get from him could solve so many of the mysteries surrounding the Lost Colony."

"Cause he's been dead for over two hundred years," Hank said.

"Oh," Nick said.

Frogs
Caribbean Islands, 1781

After the Revolution, I found myself looking for something new. So, with the spoils of the war I had accumulated, I got a ship, the Graciela, and put together a crew. The market was open for anyone willing to toss their hat in the ring to trade. Bring linen, dried fruit, flour, raw metals and fur down to the Caribbean, then bring sugar, cotton and spices back. Easy, simple and lucrative.

Made so much money I had no idea what to do with it at first. My descendants have been taken care of by the growth of those spoils to this day. Usually they never even suspect that my lawyers pad their portfolios and bank accounts.

But, inevitably, something went wrong.

One of the crew found himself in a bit of trouble with what you can call a Voodoo Priest, who was playing with forces that he knew too little about.

"Captain!" One of the crew yelled as he found me laying in a hammock strung between two Palm trees on the beach over looking the sea.

"What is it, Row?" I said without opening my eyes. I had been drifting near the dreamworld, and wasn't happy I wouldn't get closer.

"It's Smith, he stirred up some locals and they dragged him off," Row said, panting.

"What were you idiots doing?" I growled and hopped to my feet.

"Gambling on some roosters, and we won," Row said.

"Where did you come from, you're dripping sweat all over the place?" I said.

"I ran here as fast as I could," Row said. "There were to many and I couldn't stop them, it took everything I had to get away."

"Figures," I said. "Luckily you're a skilled rigger or I'd leave you here when we ship off for being a scaredy cat."

"Why fight when I can run I always say," Row said.

I turned slowly to Row, stared unblinking for a few moments then said, "You go any direction other than the one I'm walking and you're a dead man."

"Shouldn't we get more of the crew?" Row said looking over his shoulder toward the docks.

"No," I said and started walking the direction Row had come from. "And don't make me drag you there."

Row was at my side a step later.

It was easy enough to pick up the trail, I didn't even bother faking like I was tracking the kidnappers by their foot prints or anything like that. Row was so scared he wouldn't have noticed anyway.

Sadly, because I didn't want to carry Row or explain to him how I was able to run at super speeds our pace kept us at a trot. We didn't find them until close to midnight.

The islanders had made their way into the forests, through unkempt trails.

My expectations were that we would find these men holding my crewman captive for a modest ransom. But something didn't smell right.

Benjamin Pike had taught me many things, and one of those was to recognize that the cursed such as us had a distinct smell. A lingering scent of the animal that was sacrificed mixed with the human smell and a hint of lightning. That ozone smell from a good thunderstorm. Each individual inflicted like I am smells unique, but also familiar. Always mostly human with a touch of an animal and a storm.

What I caught in the air now was the opposite. It was an animal with the hint of human.

It made my blood boil.

Row was shaking now with fear, and as we inched closer to the clearing where we could see torches and hear drums being beat, I motioned for him to remain quiet.

He nodded, not blinking, eyes so wide I thought they were going to pop out of his head.

I saw it first.

I grabbed Row, covering his mouth before he could scream, and held him until he was out of breath.

I turned him so he couldn't see it any longer, looked him in the eye and whispered, "Run, get all of the men. Get to the Graciela and rig up to set sail as soon as I am back on board."

He nodded and I pulled my hand from his mouth.

Whispering, I said, "Quietly, but quickly. Do you understand?"

Row nodded and started back the way we came like a ninja through the brush.

I turned back to the clearing, and counted the men around the beast in the center of the clearing.

Twenty five of them, some beating drums, some chanting to themselves and rocking back and fourth to the beat, and a few others dancing around the beast. It was chained to a tree in the center, breathing heavily with snot dripping from its nose and saliva hanging in ropes from its mouth.

From the smell I could easily tell it once was a goat, but now it was misshapen and deformed. It was easily five hundred pounds. It was also suffocating from the chain around its neck.

A voodoo priest from my best guess, painted black and white, came from behind the animal carrying a Thurible smoking with incense, mumbling something to the beast. In his other hand was a large knife.

As I watched this, I noticed something else in the air of the rainforest of Hispaniola. Someone like me was there, and he was close by. All of my senses were on fire now, you may say they were turned past eleven.

I searched through the trees with my ears trying to find where he was, and heard a question whispered, "Henry Kelsey? Is that you?"

It was not Benjamin Pike or any other voice I immediately recognized. Without any fear that I could detect, this cursed man came to my side and looked me in the eye.

"You look exactly like your da," the cursed man said in a thick Irish accent. "But bigger."

It wasn't the face I recognized first, but his smell, and whispered, "Mr. O'Cuinn, how is this possible?"

"Same as you I suppose, burned a witch alive and a few days later during a full moon I woke up with fifty dead colonists around me," O'Cuinn said. "And I go by Quinn these days."

"What is going on?" I asked not knowing what else to do other than focus on getting my crewman back. "This looks and feels wrong but I can't tell why."

"The opposite of us was done to that animal," Quinn whispered. "Do you know anything about the people who live on this island? Where they come from or what they believe?"

"I've heard a few stories around fires and in the pubs of Port-au-Prince," I whispered.

"These men practice voodoo and are going to sacrifice that creature to their favorite spirits, or Loa," Quinn said. "The one holding the knife, he's what they call a Bokor, a sorcerer of sorts. He's well known for helping make dead slaves and trapping souls in talismans or Ouangas. He is hoping to gain better favor with his Loa by sacrificing this animal with a slice of human soul."

"How do you know all of this?" I asked.

"I love this kind of shite," Quinn said.

"What do we do?" Hank said.

"We watch and hope that he kills that abomination quickly," Quinn said. "If he doesn't we cannot let it live."

"What about the rest of them?" I asked.

"I think you know the answer to that, mate," Quinn said.

I said nothing more and turned my attention back to the scene unfolding in front of us.

Quinn, however, did not stop talking, which brought back memories from when I was a child. He would constantly be jabbering on no matter what we were doing.

"I've met a few of our kind, but never someone that I knew when either of us were just a man," Quinn said. The Bokor was still muttering and pacing around the beast with the incense. "Mind you, I pretty much killed everyone I knew. I was at Roanoke, they didn't disappear. I massacred most of them, but some were able to get away and found refuge with the natives."

The drumming was faster now, and the Bokor's chanting was more pronounced. I still couldn't tell what he was saying though.

"Do you still call Kelsey Town home?" Quinn asked.

I shook my head.

"Makes sense, that was ninety years ago," Quinn said. "I don't stay in one place more than a few years myself. Find myself back here on the Mar Caribe quite a bit though. So many come and go through these islands I'm forgotten more often than I'm remembered. Plus I love the women. Oh my are they fantastic."

The Bokor dropped the incense burner and raised the knife above his head and I could understand the two words he was chanting now, "Baron Samedi."

He repeated that over and over and over again.

"What are the odds he actually kills it?" Quinn asked.

I glanced over slowly, then back to the spectacle in front of us.

"You always were the quiet type," Quinn said.

The Bokor slashed at the beast's neck, right below where the chain was chocking it.

The voodoo man was too slow.

The beast reared, the chain strained and stretched against the creatures skin. It was able to get a noise past the binding. The sound was deep and I could feel it through the ground.

The Bokor brought the blade around again and buried it in the animals neck. The muscles were so thick that the blade got stuck in the flesh.

The beast's muscles swelled even more, and the sound of the chain snapping reverberated through the trees.

It reared its head back and let out a bleat that shook the ground.

It had doubled in size in the few moments from when the blade went in to right after the chain broke.

It snapped at the Bokor taking the man's left arm and a chunk of his upper torso with it.

The man screamed and the drumming stopped.

Other men were now screaming and the beast, well the beast was feeding.

Most of the men were easy prey, but a few of them escaped the circle.

But not for long.

The men were too slow.

I was having trouble following it through the trees in the darkness.

"That is going to be hard to catch," Quinn said. "Hopefully you're as strong as you are quiet."

I looked over at Quinn, then darted off into the forest after the beast. Without hesitation, I changed and slammed into the side of the cursed goat as hard as I could. It went through tree after tree after tree until it was finally stopped by a monster of a Silk Cotton tree older than the forest. Its roots protruding from the ground like buttresses holding up the towering toward heaven trunk.

Quinn was at my side as the beast pushed itself up. "I was hoping that smell was lingering from your days on the farm. You're about the creepiest thing I've ever seen."

I looked down at him as he smiled and laughed.

Stepping away from me, Quinn moved quickly. He had the chain in his hands, and wrapped it around the beast's throat. He was up on the creatures back, digging his heals into the nape of the creature's neck . It bleated again, low and gravely as Quinn pulled back harder.

"A little help here," Quinn said. "Our only chance is to snap its poor neck. Gotta put it out of it's misery before it goes on a rampage across the island."

Quinn was straining so hard I saw his hands change, they doubled in size and hints of the webbing showed between his fingers. Then the green ran up his arms as his muscles bulged. One moment he was an Irishman who wouldn't shut up, the next he was a giant frogman with no vocal cords.

I preferred him as a frogman.

He didn't really have a neck either, just shoulders then frog head. He had to hunch over a bit to look forward.

The chain was beginning to flex but I knew it would snap at any moment.

So, I crouched and lunged at the creature's enormous, misshapen head. Catching it's horns and using my momentum, I swung my body around with all of my might and between Quinn and I there was a great snap, and the beast fell limp into the damp floor of the rain forest.

"That was interesting," Quinn said, his head was mostly human with the rest of him following behind as he jumped down from the beast.

I considered leaving before I changed back to avoid any more small talk. But I wanted to find my crewman's body.

"These men took one of my crew," I said as I changed back. "I want to give him a proper burial at sea as he would have wanted."

"Ahhhhh, all makes sense now. We should also bury this fella," Quinn said patting the beasts side. "Let the locals think it was a sea wolf attack."

"You think they will believe a couple of seals did all of this?" Hank looked around at the carnage. There were body parts every where and the trees were painted in blood.

"Those suckers are vicious when provoked," Quinn said. "Lets find your man and get this over with. I think it's time I bid fare thee well to Hispaniola and you seem to be in need of a replacement on your crew. I can fill in on whatever job you need and I'll work for passage only, don't really need the money anymore. I'm sure you've figured out that a long life guarantees long term investment returns."

I sighed, knowing it was best to get him off the island and I didn't want to waste time searching for a new helmsman.

We buried the body of the animal below the tree where it had died. Seemed a fitting resting place for the last vessel of my helmsman's soul. We brought Smith's remains back to the ship and a few hours after setting sail, at sunset over the Caribbean Sea, we gave him a proper send off into the waves.

Quinn and I had a few more adventures after that, made a lot of money on those boats, but Quinn had this itch to fight and it got the better of him in 1811. There was a great comet that year and he decided to throw his hat into the arena at the Tournament. In his third fight, against a manticore, it stung him with its scorpion tail over and over until Quinn was paralyzed. Quinn could do nothing to stop the manticore as it breathed its fire, killing my friend.

Chapter 8

"Is this an autobiography since you're just a tool?" Hank said as he picked up a log from the pile next to him.

"You're hilarious," Nick said. "Why don't you tell me about the night you were cursed?"

"I don't think so," Hank said as he dropped the log onto the fire.

"Fine," Nick said. "Now I know you connected with Ben and this Quinn, are there any other Were creatures that come to mind that you might want to talk about?"

"Yes," Hank said. "Her name was Josephine."

"The rare female Were creature," Nick said. "What year was this?"

"1849, and I had found myself in San Francisco," Hank said.

"You were a Forty-niner?" Nick perked up.

"No, I was keeping my head down, importing goods from the East Coast that people longed for, running some table games and offering a room to sleep it off," Hank said. "Then she walked into my place and ruined everything."

Hate To Feel
San Francisco - 1849

I was running my shop in Portsmouth Square, part of China Town now, in San Francisco. It was where the first American Flag was raised after the city was taken, known then as Yerba Buena, by Captain John Berrien Montgomery of the U.S.S. Portsmouth.

I had gotten there about eight or so months before the rush.

Kind of wish I had left as soon as Samuel Brannan went running up and down the square shouting about gold for the taking out on the American River. The very next day, people started flooding the city. My business expanded quickly as more and more people from the East Coast wanted something to remind them of home. These pan handlers started having a few bucks in their pockets and would easily pay double for their favorite chocolate, whiskey or a newspaper from home. Soon enough, I owned the building I was in and decided to start renting out the rooms up stairs.

You could come in, get your favorite whiskey and sleep off the effects. More often than not, these men were looking for company and would wander in with one of the night walkers that were following all the fortune seekers into the city. It wasn't my place to judge these women or men for their choices, even though it was very tempting, I never took them onto my own pay roll. I let them make their money, but also protected my guests. So, I opened my safe to deposits from the patrons because they were very easy targets when they were drunk and happy. And I wanted to make sure they could pay their bill.

Every few days I would catch one of these women rolling one of my guests who had a tough time waking up the next morning and I would ban her from my establishment.

Gambling was a way of life in the early days of San Fran, and I had a few tables with more or less trust worthy dealers working for me. It wasn't very fun for me. But, it was easy and I did find myself keeping a running bet with a few of the other merchants in the square concerning the special guests of my patrons. It was becoming a weekly occurrence that I would have to ban a girl for trying to sneak off with one of my patrons hard earned cash. Usually a new girl who hadn't quite learned the difference between my place and the others in the city. And we would bet on which night of the week I would find myself tossing a girl out on her butt.

As I said, most of these places had their own girls working, or had a mutually beneficial arrangement with a few local girls and those running them. So, me banning a girl only helped them out. Made their place more desirable with less hassle for those looking to make a quick buck. It improved my position with patrons who had a bit more money lining their pockets and they were willing to pay to protect it. My tables were always filled and my rooms were turning over less and less.

A few dozen banned girls later, I thought my reputation had spread enough that I wouldn't have to deal with the stupidity of thieves any longer.

But one night, a new girl walked in on the arm of a man who recently made a big find. His luck was starting to run out though. He had checked most of his stake in with me, but had been showing off around some of the other joints that evening. And this new girl wanted whatever she could dig out of his pockets.

An hour later, I was walking to my room. I heard him snoring and her going though his pockets. I stood outside of the door, a bit sad that this was going to have to happen, and opened the door.

The girl immediately screamed, but my guest didn't even stir.

"What is your name?" I said quietly.

"Don't come anywhere near me," she said and pulled out a knife.

"You haven't been in this city very long," I said. "But thieves are not tolerated here. The best you can do, is to put back what wasn't paid to you for your services, leave and never come back."

"You gonna make me?" she said and pulled out a small dagger.

"I would rather not," I answered but she lunged at me with the knife anyway. I easily took it out of her hand and buried it in the wall with a quick toss. I flipped her upside down, shook her to see what might fall out the hiding places in her dress and watched as no less than eight knives bounced off the floor with two of them sticking into the wood perfectly. A few coins and a good chunk of gold bounced off the floor as well.

She kicked and she screamed and I just stood there. None of the others had ever put up this much of a fight. I placed her over my shoulder as I knelt down to pick up a coin, I can't remember exactly, but it was pretty much the standard fare for her services.

As I stood up I placed her back on her feet, she was still throwing punches, turned her around and walked her with a bit of persuasion past all the tables. This act of shaming served two purposes. The guests and my employees saw the girls face and the other companions saw that I was fair but stern.

She spit in my face.

I wiped my face off. Then she spat curses of every variety as I handed her the coin I picked up a few minutes earlier and smiled as I told her, "Please do not ever come into my establishment again. I wouldn't wish for you to lose any more clients on account of my business policies."

She sneered at me, spat in my face once more then turned on her heal and marched away.

I cleaned myself up and added my guests recovered property to what I had in his deposit box in my safe.

The next morning he was pleasantly surprised to find that he hadn't gambled or drank away his spending cash and thanked me for my services. His pride was a bit fragile and he decided to head out that day and get back to work on the river. He wished to utilize my services further concerning his money and we worked out a deal.

Later that day, my door opened. When I looked up from the front desk where I was leaning reading the paper, a woman I had never seen walked in wearing a dress as fine as I had ever seen. Her skin was like chocolate, her eyes were so dark you got lost in your own head looking into them and she smelled like flowers and the cursed.

"Hello good sir," she said. He voice flowing off her tongue like she could have anything. The twitch of her nose gave away that she knew I wasn't just a slick business man exploiting those seeking their fortunes like everyone else raising gambling halls toward the sky in that town.

"How do you do ma'am?" I asked. "And what might your name be?"

Her eyes darted to the shadows of the room. She didn't know I could follow such quick and slight movements, leading me to believe she was young, and hadn't ever run across another like us before.

Inside I smiled because I thought this was going to be fun.

I was horribly mistaken.

"My name is Josephine Monroe," she said and looked me right in the eye from across the front desk. Then she extended her hand to me.

"Very nice to meet you, Miss Monroe," I said and shook her hand. "My name is Henry Kelsey. Welcome to my place. What can I help you with?"

"I have heard a great deal about you, Mr. Kelsey," She said looking around the room. "And I am here to offer you an opportunity to grow your business."

"And what opportunity would that be?" I asked. I could also smell the girl from the night before, the one that tried to steal from my guest, on her. I knew exactly what she was. She was an aspiring Madam. Smart to use her abilities like that if she could control herself, not worth the risk in my book.

"I am hoping to expand upon your current policy on girls working in your place," she said.

"I'm perfectly happy letting them work as long as my guests feel safe with their belongings on my property," I said.

"Have you ever wondered how much one of these girls can make in an evening?" Josephine said.

"I know exactly how much they can make," I said. "Do you?"

"Are you implying that my girls aren't honest and proper young ladies?" Josephine asked.

"Not at all," I said. I pulled out my pocket watch and checked the time. "Oh, but that reminds me, I have a meeting in an hour with Sasquatch."

"Well, I will only keep you a few more moments then," she sighed audibly and visibly. "I want to offer you a partnership. My girls are the best earners around. And it would be much easier for us to move into a place like this, rather than build my own."

"I guess my reputation hasn't proceeded me," I said.

"On the contrary," Josephine said. "You run the tightest ship in the city, and that interests me. What do you call this place by the way."

"I don't call it anything, and business beyond my current dealings do not interest me," I said. "But you and your girls are welcome to come back anytime and enjoy yourselves. As long as everyone keeps their hands in their own pockets."

"You just might see me later on this evening, then, Mr. Kelsey," she said and smiled. Then she turned and walked out of my place. I didn't even have an actual name for it, never got around to getting a sign.

I have no idea what I did the rest of the day an hour later a few more visitors walked through my door.

"Hello, Kelsey," the mouthpiece of the group said as he walked in.

"Good afternoon, twat," I said. His name was Luther Black. He was a twat.

"Always so inviting," Luther said.

"I didn't invite you in here," I said.

"Well, we have a few things that we need to discuss," Luther said.

"No we don't," I said.

"We know that beast of woman approached you about a partnership," Luther said.

"And?" I said.

"Are you going to accept her offer?" One of the other men asked.

"How much will it piss you off if I do?" I asked.

"That's not the answer we were looking for," Luther said and shook his head.

"It's not your business," I said. "So piss off."

"You understand that she runs some of the most aggressive and lucrative girls in the city?" Another guy said.

"And?" I said. "She can keep on doing that as she pleases. My guests are welcome to bring anyone they wish into my joint, and I'll make sure my guests have all of their belongings when they check out. Well, whatever they didn't lose to my tables that is."

"That's not going to work for us any more either," Luther said. The whole group mumbled and nodded in agreement.

"What does it matter to you if I let them peddle their wares and don't take a cut?" I said. "It's only my financial loss."

"No, Mr. Kelsey," Luther said. "We've all lost girls to Ms. Monroe and if you would finally join us we could work against her more efficiently."

"You fellas having that tough of a time dealing with this little lady?" I laughed.

"She's not what she seems, Kelsey," Luther said.

"She broke the arm of one of my dealers," one of the guys yelled.

"He probably deserved it," I said.

"And her girls are twice as sneaky and even more ruthless than any of the other independents in the city," Luther said.

"You could stop letting them in," I said. "Or stop being twats."

"That's not an option for us," Luther said. "Not without everyone in the square on the same page. Strength in unity, Mr. Kelsey."

I stood up straight at that comment, looked around the room and said, "I don't work well with others."

Luther shook his head, "Not the answer we are looking for."

The whole group turned around knowing that their fight was lost, and walked out the door.

That night my tables were packed and I was booked solid for the evening. No less than eight of Josephine's girls were on the laps of my guests or in their beds. I quickly did the math and it was a lot of money I was giving up by seeing my daughters faces on everyone of those girls who walked in with one of my guests. I wasn't going to judge them for their chosen profession, but I just couldn't take money from them that they earned. The rooms they were sharing and the drinks they were drinking were paid for. So who was I to say they had to give me a cut.

As you may guess from the conversation with Luther, I wasn't well liked in the city because of my perspective. They had tried to beat a lesson into my skull a few months earlier, but that backfired on them. They may not have liked me or the way I conducted business, but their fear out weighed their distaste. I crippled three of the ten men they sent after me. One of them was Luther's bastard. They were lucky I didn't kill any of them.

It was close to two in the morning when Josephine walked through my door again. She looked me right in the eye, I was behind the bar, and she walked right to me.

"Well hello Ms. Monroe," I said. "Can I get you a drink?"

"I would love a bottle of whiskey," she said.

"Would you like a glass to go along with that bottle?" I asked.

"Two," she said.

I grabbed a bottle of the only one I would drink and two glasses. I put the glasses down and uncorked the bottle.

"Put the bottle down, Mr. Kelsey," she said before I could pour our drinks.

I placed the bottle on the bar.

Smiling, she picked up the bottle and poured two very healthy glasses. She put the bottle down, picked up one glass and said, "Bottoms up."

"No toast?" I said.

"Toasts are for people who enjoy lying in front of crowds," she said as I picked up my glass. She clinked hers to mine, then put the glass to her lips.

I followed suit, and we kept eye contact as we drained our glasses.

As we both placed our glasses on the bar it hit me. She was cursed and it was easy placing the way she smelled - musky and Earthy and wild. She was an honest to goodness real life Werewolf.

"You and I both know this will take a very long time and at least half your bar to get us drunk," Josephine said.

"Oh, I'd say about a third if we drink it real quick," I said.

"I know you're not like the rest of the men in this city, Mr. Kelsey," she said. "I just can't figure out what."

"What makes you say that, Ms. Monroe?" I said. I could just tell her everything I knew, but it was more fun watching her struggle with the questions she wanted to ask.

"I know you can sense that I'm not like the rest of the women in this city," she said. "I can see it in the way you move, like you're trying to be gentle with the glass your holding so you don't crush it. And the way you smell, we live in a city but the air around you is perfumed with the country and the farm and something very familiar."

"Are you saying I stink?" I smiled.

"Quite the opposite, it is intoxicating to be around someone that has the same underlying fragrance."

"Interesting," I said.

Faster than anyone in the room could register, Josephine hopped the bar sliding between me and the wood. Pressed against me with her tongue found my mouth quickly. She pushed me toward the stairs as her hands roamed my shoulders and chest and arms. I kissed her back, but pointed to one of my guys to keep their eyes open while I entertain my lady friend up stairs.

I turned away from her, but took her hand at the bottom of the stairs. We walked up quickly to my room and as soon as my door was closed, Josephine ripped my shirt and vest right off me.

I grabbed her and pulled her to me. She pushed against me, testing her own strength, but I was far more powerful than she was.

I undid the back of her dress easily and stripped it off. Her corset took a few seconds more, but she was quickly only half dressed same as me.

In a flash though, she had my pants off.

That was the first time I had slept with another cursed like I am. It was certainly unique and more intense than any physical relationship I ever had.

We collapsed into the bed, which had also collapsed, more spent than I had been since becoming what I was.

"You might be the palest man I have ever bedded," Josephine said, still panting with sweat beading on every inch of her dark skin, looking over our bodies. I was on my back and she was draped over me with her head resting on my chest.

"Palest something, but certainly not a man," I said.

Josephine raised her head up and looked into my eyes and asked, "What are you then?"

"I'm cursed, just like you," I said.

"You don't think we're human anymore?" she said.

"No man or woman has ever lived for 175 years aside from poorly translated passages from the Old Testament," I said.

"Who did this to you?" she asked.

"A witch, same as you," I said.

"Why?" she asked.

"That's not something I want to talk about," I slide out from under her and put my feet on the floor. "

"Please don't go," she said. "I have never met anyone like us."

"I have to piss," I said and stood up. I looked over my shoulder at Josephine, "But I'll be right back."

I went into the adjoining room, filled my chamber pot and looked out the window. The streets were quiet, dawn wasn't far off and everyone was either asleep or dead.

I walked back into the other room and Josephine was almost dressed.

"You don't have to go," I said.

"I want to go," she said and stepped closer to me, "But I want to come back."

I nodded.

Josephine smiled, leaned in and kissed me.

I grabbed her around the waist and pulled her into my arms kissing her back.

"Will you tell me what you become at the full moon before I go?" She asked.

"No," I said.

She looked down and pushed away from me.

"But you can see in three days if you want to join me out on the island that I have been using to keep the people in the city safe from me," I said.

"That's what you do?" Her eyes widened. "I've been taking to the mountains."

"Most of our kind does it's best to isolate themselves during that time," I said.

"Makes business a bit more difficult," Josephine said.

"To say the least," I said.

Josephine smiled, but her attention quickly turned toward the window. She sniffed the air, then looked back to me. "Do you smell that? "

I took a deep breath through my nose and knew instantly what it was. I bolted out the door and down the stairs as a flaming bottle came crashing through the front window of my place. It hit the front desk, sending little fires spreading across the wood. Then more bottles came through the windows all around me.

"FIRE!" I roared as loud as I could. Doors swung open from the second floor. Most of them stopped dead in their tracks at the site of a large naked man screaming fire but they quickly snapped out of it and scrambling feet flew down the stairs.

"Out the back!" I bellowed as whores and Johns ran past me.

I closed my eyes and listened. There were too many heartbeats and footfalls for me to get a lock on one of the arsonists. My only chance was to go out the front and catch the scent of whomever did this.

Smoke was filling the place, I couldn't see the second floor railing any longer and the fire was climbing the front wall.

Josephine came down the stairs through the smoke looking to me.

I had only a small chance of catching who did this, and since she could safely get out the back, I took off through the fire that had engulfed the front of my place.

I don't suggest jumping through a raging fire with no clothes on, even if you heal almost instantly. It hurt.

I gritted my teeth and found a familiar scent in the air. Luther Black mixed with lamp oil.

I took off after the trail, and it turned out Luther was as slow as he was stupid.

I caught him in an alley a few doors down from my place.

Men were getting buckets of water and dousing the flames now. They may save the buildings from burning around mine, but my place was going to burn to the ground.

I was not happy.

I grabbed Luther by the shoulders and tossed him against one of the buildings. I held back and he bounced off the wall and fell to his hands and knees in front of me.

Luther looked up at me, blood and drool pouring from his mouth and tears welling up in his eyes.

"Henry, please," Luther mumbled as he scrambled to his feet. "I... I didn't--"

I grabbed him by the throat and lifted him off the ground. I pulled him close and looked him in the eyes.

I watched for a few moments as he struggled to breath and his eyes started to bulge. I grabbed onto the top of his head, my hand now twice the size of a mans with two inch long claws that dug into his skull.

Deliberately squeezing with one hand and yanking with the other, Luther's head tore from his neck. Blood sprayed the wall, my face and my chest. The only noise coming from him was the ripping flesh and the splash of his blood.

I dropped the body into the dirt at my feet. Then brought Luther's head close to mine and looked in his vacant eyes. I spit in his face and dropped his head in the dirt next to his body.

I turned to find Josephine watching me. Her eyes were big and bright; possibilities she hadn't imagined were sparking and catching fire just like my place.

We stood there for a moment, I wasn't planning on saying anything when she asked, "What do we do now?"

"I need a bath," I said. I reached down and shook Luther's body free of his coat. Luckily it had been a chilly evening so he was wearing a long coat. I slid it on and buttoned it up.

"Pants might also be a good idea," she said. "But I mean grand scheme of things idea, not exact next step."

"Always one step at a time," I said and started back toward the raging fire that used to be my place. I walked past not even looking over at the inferno and headed for the bay.

Close on my heels, Josephine asked, "Where are we going?"

"Bath," I said and picked up the pace to something a bit more supernatural, and Josephine matched my speed. At the water, I tossed the coat aside and walked into the bay.

"You were serious," Josephine said from the water's edge.

I glared at her as I scrubbed off the blood.

"There were others, why don't we go hunt all of them down too?" Josephine said.

"I killed the only one that mattered," I said as I walked out of the water. The water was evaporating off of my skin in the brisk air and it looked to me as if I was smoldering. Memories of running through the forest near my home flashed in my head, of rain turning to steam as it hit my over heating skin. But I shook off those memories as they wouldn't help me right then.

"We could take out all of your competition and run the whole city! Who would stand against you after what they just did?" She said.

"They aren't my competition anymore," I said and picked the coat off of the ground.

"You're just going to give up?" She said.

"You can go exact all the revenge you wish," I said as I slid the coat on. "I got mine."

"But think of all the money you could make by taking all of them down," she said.

"You think I need the money after all these years? All these lifetimes! I run a business every few years hoping to feel a little bit human again," I said and started back toward the square.

"We're better than they are!" She screamed.

"No, we're more broken," I said. "Those witches made sure of that."

"Are you just going to disappear then? Just run off and hide?" She ran up next to me and asked.

"I'm going crack open my safe then get a little lost," I said. "You are welcome to join me if you wish."

"But I have a business to run," She said. "I can't just abandon my girls."

"You can do whatever you wish," I said. "They'll find their own way. Easy for women to sell what God gave them in this horrendous place."

"So you just want me to go run wild with you in the wilderness?" she asked.

"I was thinking head North, I've heard good things about the Redwoods," I said.

"Redwoods? Seriously?" she said, shook her head and walked off to who knows where.

I didn't say anything else, I just headed to Portsmouth Square.

The sun was peaking over the hills now and my place was rubble. A few of the main supports were still standing, charred and smoking. Everything around my place was intact, a few scorch marks on the two buildings next to mine, but nothing compromising their integrity.

"Holy hell Hank, thank God you're alive," one of my dealers yelled when he saw me.

"I am alive, William," I said.

"More than I can say for that snake Luther," William said. "Found torn in half down the street."

"Pissed someone off did he?" I asked.

"Pissed something off all right," William said and looked me right in the eye.

William was pretty sharp and I trusted him to take care of my place when I needed to go away for business once a month. We never discussed it, but a few decades later, I found myself at his deathbed and he just smiled when he saw I hadn't aged a day after the last time he had seen me. Which would be the morning after the fire.

"I need you to do something for me, William," I said.

"Of course, what do you need?" William asked.

"Rebuild for me," I said. "I'll leave you with enough to get running. And take in Josephine and her girls if she is still interested in a partnership."

"Where ya going, boss?" William said.

"I'm going to go see if there is any money to be made up north," I said. "Getting to crowded for me he in San Fran."

"When ya think yer comin' back?" William asked.

"Don't think I am, William," I said. "But I will keep in touch. I'll have everything set up for you in the next few hours."

I spent the rest of the morning collecting every cent I had in the city and getting a new suit. I had William named as my executor for all legal and property matters in the city.

I thought about tracking Josephine down, but that wasn't really in my nature. So I made my way out to the island I had been using to deal with the full moon.

Part of me hoped that Josephine would show up on the full moon, but

I mostly wished to be left alone.

When the moon rose above the water, huge and tugging at my insides, I started to let myself get lost in the change. I shook and sweat and every muscle in my body tensed. My hands changed first as I fell to my knees in the grass. I looked up at the moon, hating that I couldn't stop it, and out of the corner of my eye I saw a beautiful, reddish wolf snarling at me from the tree line. She smelled of flowers and musky and Earthy and wild.

"You little heartbreaker you," I said through gritted teeth as the curse took over.

Chapter 9

"So, Josephine broke the heart of a witch," Nick said. "Did not see that one coming."

"We ended up spending the next year traveling from camp to camp between California and what was to become Alaska," Hank said.

"Did you ever find out her cursed story?" Nick asked.

"I wouldn't ask a woman about her past romances as I'm not going to discuss my past courtships with them."

"What happened to her then?" Nick asked. "Is she still alive?"

"She got sick of me," Hank said. "Last I heard she was a Studio Exec in Hollywood or something."

"Seriously?" Nick cocked his head, intrigued.

"Yeah, so?" Hank said.

"We should get your life story up on the big screen," Nick said.

"I hate you," Hank said.

"Come on it would be great," Nick said. "We could get Brad Pitt to play you and Bradley Cooper for me."

"Why the hell would you be in it?" Hank asked.

"As your biographer," Nick said.

"No, the story would only be about my adventures, not us sitting here talking about it," Hank said.

"I'm pretty sure I've been on an adventure or two with you," Nick said. "Did you forget about the Beaver Hat or all those times you've managed to get yourself hammered and needed me to drive you home?"

"The Beaver Hat story is pretty solid, but everything else you've done with me is boring," Hank said.

"Wow, way to trivialize our thirty years of friendship."

"Don't be such a pansy," Hank said.

"Why don't you finally tell me about the night you were cursed then?" Nick said.

"No," Hank said and flicked the Zippo open with his thumb.

"Then what do you want to talk about?"

"Nothing," Hank said flicking the lighter closed and crossed his arms.

"Who's being a pansy now?" Nick asked.

Narrowing his eyes, Hank said, "I want to tell you about going to war again," Hank said.

"Which war?" Nick asked.

"The Great Rebellion," Hank said. "The one you call the Civil War."

Man In the Box
Virginia, April 1863

War is a hell of a drug.

For some men it is more potent than coke or heroin.

It is extremely intoxicating when your blood is boiling with rage as the full moon pulls on the souls inside your skin.

Cursed men like me were on both sides of that war. I, like the few I know, were there because we wanted to preserve the country. I had been at its founding and didn't want something as petty as ownership of another human to ruin what so many of my friends died for.

Hell, I still get annoyed when I see these idiots waving Confederate Battle flags. Think they are rebels when in fact they are just pissy little babies supporting pissy little rich Southern babies who wanted to bring their pet humans to their vacation homes in the North. But the Northern States expressed their State's Right to outlaw owning or transporting slaves and the secessionists threw a tantrum that cost hundreds of thousands of lives.

Obviously, I fought for the Union Army and my skills at tracking and scouting had me in a position where I worked alone a great deal of the time. Made it easier to use my gifts and not be noticed.

I was with a unit in Virginia in the end of April near a town called Chancellorsville under Major General Joseph Hooker. The next few days would see one of the bloodiest battles of that war.

Robert E. Lee was commanding the Confederate Army of Northern

Virginia. When General Lee realized he was out numbered two to one, he split his forces. A move that was not a popular choice among his men, but ultimately lead to a Confederate victory. General Hooker mistook his position and multiple timid decisions proved insufficient against the audacity of the Confederate General's tactics.

We, the Union Army, had suffered a loss that evening as Lt. Gen. Stonewall Jackson ambushed us from the woods in the late afternoon.

The woods were very quiet much of the day as the wildlife tend to run from the commotion that comes with an army marching through. Stupidly, I had mistaken the movement of the forest animals, thinking it was because of our own companies maneuvers when in fact it was because of the approaching Rebel forces creeping through the woods. We were forced to retreat and regroup.

On the night of the full moon, I found myself out in the forest under the excuse that I was on watch for any scouting or raiding parties. The air was still thick with the smell of blood from the ambush. Each man who died was distinct in the air and their faces shot through my mind every time I closed my eyes. My insides were tied in knots as I tried to push my senses harder than I had ever before at that point. I was hoping to use the full moon to my advantage in preventing any further attacks under the moonlight and maybe just maybe put the fear of God into those traitorous gray backs.

I moved easily through the brush making my way to the Confederate line. What I found was more than I could have hoped. Stonewall Jackson was moving out of his camp on a scouting mission. Easily, I flanked him and his men watching as they made their way on the Plank Road.

From a safe distance, he surveyed the Union camp, and I could see the smile on his face. That was the smile of a commander that had a plan. From what I could see, my mind raced with possible strategies for attack and came to the conclusion that every option Jackson had under the heavy moonlight would be a guaranteed victory for Jackson and his men. 217

That's when I lost it.

Jackson and his men heard me before they saw me. To their credit, they quickly recognized me as a threat and were able to get a shot off. I vaguely remember taking the bullet to the shoulder, but it slowed me down enough for them to make a break for the furthest lines of their men. I was on their tail, taking one of Jackson's guards out of the equation as they reached firing distance from their frontline.

Not understanding what they were seeing, the Grey backs fired as their commander galloped toward them. I can't know what they were thinking but in the commotion I was wounded once more.

But so was Lt. Gen. Stonewall Jackson.

Reading the history books, the story that comes from that night is slightly different than the pieces I remember through the change and the pain and the smell of blood.

According to the accounts of Jackson's men, they believed his scouting party was Union Cavalry taking advantage of the moonlight. Jackson would lose his left arm to amputation, it was buried the next morning. He lost his life a little over a week later because of pneumonia. I don't know where he was buried, but whenever I'm in Virginia I make it a point to go and laugh over the grave of his arm at the Ellwood Manor family cemetery.

The Union army would lose the Battle of Chancellorsville, but with the death of Stonewall Jackson, the next great battle at Gettysburg would go a much different direction because of his absence.

Chapter 10

"I think that is the first time I have ever heard you use the words 'I made a mistake' since I met you," Nick said.

"Fuck you," Hank said and drained his beer.

"Whatever, progress is progress," Nick said and laughed. "Do you need another prompt or will you tell me the story I want to hear?"

Hank did his best impression of a statue again, his eyes trained on the fire burning bright and warm between he and Nick. The flames that danced in his eyes was the only thing that gave away that he was flesh as his breath was so slow it was imperceptible in the night air around the fire.

"Just sit there and listen," Hank said. The air had grown a bit colder behind them. "No prompts, no sarcastic comments, no back and forth. But I want you to think about these three question while I tell this story. Do you remember where every creature you sentenced to death is buried? Do you remember every promise you have made? And are the tally's even close to equal on both."

Nick kept his mouth shut and sat on the hammock perfectly still.

Would?
Kelseytown Connecticut October, 1986

Benjamin and I sat around this same fire a few nights before he was killed. He told me that someone needed to take care of Penny.

"One of us has to do this," Benjamin said. "I will try but I don't know if I'm too much of a monster now to do it right, Henry."

"And you think I can do it?" I said "Are you out of your crusty brain!"

"You have dealt with being what we are much better than I could ever have and you now have this relationship with Nicholas, you're doing exactly what I want to do for Penny with him right now!" Ben said.

"Let's get through the next few days, Ben, survive this battle ahead of us, and we will talk more about this," I said.

"That is exactly why we need to make this decision now, Henry!" Ben said. "There is a chance one of us won't survive what is coming," Ben said.

"There is a chance we will all die," I said. "So why worry about such a small decision until we get through this fight?"

"Because it is important to me, Henry," Ben said. "I need to know someone will help her if I'm not here anymore to try. More important to me than anything I can remember since I have become this creature, since the curse."

"More important than your beaver hats?" I said and chuckled.

"Much more important Henry. Penny needs someone to give her structure, to let her know she isn't alone, someone she can depend on. She hasn't ever had that, and she will need and she deserves that."

"I don't think I'm the guy to give her structure or a home, Ben, and I certainly don't think you're in a place to do that. You spend most of your days on the bottom of the ocean chasing giant squid and Great Whites."

"And If I survive I will try and put that behind me, but I don't know if I can. That is why I need your help if I do, or if I don't survive, I need you to promise you will try."

"Nick and Mina will be around, they can help you or take care of her," I said.

"First, they are fifteen years old and won't be able to take in a ward for a few more years. Second, they may be part of our world, but they are much more human than they are one of us!"

"Penny isn't a monster," I said. "She's a child, just a little girl."

"Penny isn't human at all," Ben said. "Don't let the form she shows us most fool you, Henry, you know better than that. She has lived her entire life, all nine years, as a monster. Death and killing has been a part of her whole life, it has filled all of her moments awake, it fills her dreams and it permeates her memory. If she isn't helped now, she could become very dangerous and do you want Nick and Mina to be forced to make a decision later about Penny's life that you and I could have at least tried to avoid?"

"You think Mina would ever hurt that child?"

"I know when it comes down to it, if that child grows up to have no care or worry for the mortal world, Nick and Mina will do what their ancestors have always done. They will protect the weaker of the two."

The fire crackled in front of us. Embers danced above the flames where the heat mixed with the crisp October air. I watched them float into the clear, starry sky and took a deep breath.

"I promise. But I will most likely fail."

Ben watched the same fire a few moments before he said, "Thank you."

A few days later he sacrificed himself so that we had the time to dismember Frank Stone and spread his patchwork body across the world while you, Nick, tossed Stone's head into that volcano.

Then you Nick, Mina, Penny and I buried Ben here, on my property below one of the great Maples on the other side of the field behind us.

As we stood there, none of us knowing what to say, covered in dirt and sweat, Penny reached up with her little hand and took mine. I was never more afraid of her than that moment. But I knew she wouldn't grow up to be a monster.

I saw to that.

Killer Is Me

Chapter 11

"You did right by Penny and Ben," Nick said quietly.

"I said no back and forth, no comments, just listen," Hank said.

"Understood," Nick said.

"Give me one of your stupid cues," Hank growled. "Quickly."

"You also said no prompts," Nick said.

"Ah fuck you, just give me a stupid prompt," Hank growled.

"You've told me about going around the U.S., two war stories and a bit of island hopping in the Caribbean, but where else have you been?" Nick asked and a slight smile appeared on his face.

"'I've been everywhere man,'" Hank sang gruffly.

"Did you just answer vaguely with a Johnny Cash lyric?" Nick asked.

"I answered vaguely with a Geoff Mack lyric, idiot," Hank said and looked down at the brass lighter in his left hand.

"Who the hell is Geoff Mack?" Nick asked.

"He's an Australian Country singer. Got his start singing to the troops during WWII," Hank said.

"Is this going to be another war story?" Nick asked.

"No, I was just answering your stupid question," Hank said wrapping his fingers around the Zippo and looked back to the fire.

"There are no stupid questions," Nick said.

"Yes there are and they are always asked by people who say there are no stupid questions," Hank said.

"Whatever," Nick said. "Why did you bring up that lyric by that particular singer?"

"He wrote that song about me."

"Seriously?" Nick said. "Johnny Cash covered a song written about you?"

"Yeah, but the original was about my time in Australia," Hank said.

"What year were you living in Australia?" Nick asked.

"Not entirely sure on the years, but it was right at the end of WWII," Hank said. "I had met a woman. And if you've been paying attention, that always ends in disaster."

Sea of Sorrow
South Pacific - 1945

The ship I was on had been sunk by the Japanese and a handful of us had survived.

I had joined up with the Navy out of boredom and ended up deployed to the South Pacific. And maybe I had hoped that this would finally get the better of me. Not that I wanted all those other men to die, but I was so tired at that point and nothing else had killed me. So, I figured why not take the chance.

Sadly, it didn't kill me and my survival instincts kicked in. I vaguely remember fighting a shark, wish I could tell you that story, but it's all a blur. I was able to save two of my shipmates and get us onto a deserted island.

We had been out to sea for two weeks when we were attacked. And the full moon was coming so I knew I had to get some distance from these two men or my efforts of saving them would have been in vain. There was plenty of food on the island. Tons of fruit and the fishing was easy once I taught them how to make a basket net. We had explored every inch of that island and came to the conclusion that we were the only people to ever have stepped foot on it, and no one would ever be coming to rescue us.

I couldn't leave it at that.

So, I just started swimming the morning of the full moon. My hopes were to get far enough away from them that I wouldn't accidentally kill them and maybe stumble across a ship that could rescue them. When night fell I was far enough away to let the change take me with no worry. But I wasn't expecting to cross paths with the exact Japanese Matsu-class destroyer that had sunk the boat I had been on.

I woke up on the deck of the ship, and it looked as though the deck had been marinated in blood. I had to grab onto the railing and steady myself as not to slip in the mess. No vibration or hum of the Diesel engines, so I knew the boat was adrift, at the mercy of the tides.

I got to the first door leading below deck and listened for any noise of survivors. I couldn't hear a single heartbeat, or breath or footfall. The over powering scent of fuel and the blood and the ocean made it impossible to smell anything else.

Bits and pieces came back to me like usual as I took each step slowly down the stairs below deck. I had seen the ship before I had changed and knew exactly who they were. It caused an anger inside of me like I had not experienced before. I climbed aboard easily, and took out three of the crewmen who were up on deck. Much of the blood I had just been slipping in was theirs. I had not been quiet in killing them and more crewmen came to investigate the commotion.

I tore through every sailor that came up on deck, tossing their bits and pieces to the frenzy of sharks that had congregated around the boat. The first few bodies were chum calling every predator in the water. I vaguely remember what could only have been the Captain making sounds that seemed like begging before I bit through his neck. I spit the chunks out over the starboard side of the boat before tossing his body to the sharks, piece by piece.

I reached the crew quarters and couldn't remember anything else but flashes from the night before. Not that I wanted to anyway.

What I wanted was to clean up and put on some clothes. I prayed that there had been at least one freakishly large crewman on that boat, but was disappointed to find the largest pair of pants fit like capri's.

I then went to work getting the engines back online. I wouldn't be able to pilot this ship alone, but I could scuttle it. If I got the engines running as hot as possible then cut off the coolant tanks, they should blow and hopefully that would be enough to breach the hull. It was speculation, I knew nothing about these Japanese boats, but a Diesel engine was a Diesel engine and if it blows the ship would be out of commission for at least a little while and useless in the war for that time.

The engine room was humming, and I found an axe and buried it in the closest coolant line.

That's when I heard the cry for help.

In English.

Well, the closest an Australian can get to English.

"Seriously?" I closed my eyes.

The engine was screaming now and it was hard to discern over the noise but it was definitely a woman shrieking.

"How did I miss that?" I followed the screaming and not far from engineering there was a small storage room.

I shook my head as I unlocked it.

The screaming turned into pleading, "Please, don't hurt me anymore! Please just let me go. I don't want to die here, not like this."

I wrapped my fingers around the handle, but didn't pull. "I'm here to help you, miss. My name is Hank."

"Where the hell did a bloody American come from?" Her voice got stone cold sober.

"America," I said opening the door. "How did a Sheila get trapped in a closet on a Japanese destroyer?"

"Your accent is terrible," she said as her eyes moved over me, almost imperceptibly.

"What is your name, lady?" I asked. "And are you hurt?""

"Matilda," she said as she pushed past me out the door. "And no."

I turned and watched Matilda walk toward engineering which was rumbling now.

She looked in then turned to me and yelled over the noise, "You did this didn't you?"

I didn't say anything.

"How are we supposed to get anywhere now?" She screamed as she walked toward me.

"Lifeboat."

"We're hundreds of miles from anywhere populated idiot." She punched me in the chest then headed up the closest ladder.

I followed her up to the deck where it was slightly quieter.

"You really expect us to be able to row our way to a safe harbor?" Matilda yelled.

"I was only expecting to have to row my own butt to safety before you started yelling for help."

"How did you plan to do that?" She said. "If you don't die from thirst most likely the sun will cook your tiny little brain to a nice seared medium well before you reach dry land."

"Let's put some distance between us and this bomb because I have no idea what kind of damage I did or what might happen because of that lack of knowledge."

"Good idea from an idiot," Matilda said and headed for the stern where there was one life boat.

"Lucky for us there is at least one," I said as I picked the boat up by myself and lowered it into the water by the rope attached to it's mooring cleat.

"You're stronger than you look," Matilda said lowering a rope ladder over the side of the ship to the dingy. She was working very hard to keep me in the corner of her eye while she did that.

"I'll head down first and weigh the rope down in the boat," I said and hopped over the rail. I didn't even bother with the ladder. I landed easily and quietly in the boat.

Matilda looked down from the Destroyer with fire in her eyes, then yelled, "Don't get handsy when I get close to the boat. I can handle myself."

"Of course you can," I yelled up to her as she climbed over the rail.

She made her way slowly but efficiently down the rope ladder and hopped into the boat.

She looked up to me and said, "I hope your stamina matches your booshit strength."

"It's not bullshit," I pulled the oars from under the benches.

"Not cow crap, booshit," Matilda laughed. "As in ridiculous."

"Booshit is how you people murder the word bullshit," I sat down and slid the oars into the hooks.

"They do sound pretty similar," Matilda said and sat down in the boat.

I started rowing and quickly put distance between the ship and our little dingy. Smoke was rising from every opening of The Japanese Destroyer. Matilda watched me intently but gave no impression of being anything other than curious about me. I stopped rowing when we were about a thousand yards out and figured we were a safe distance if there were to be any explosions.

We sat there watching in silence for about ten minutes when over the now tolerable hum of the engines there was a scraping of metal on metal and a final, dull clattering noise. The engines were seized and quiet, but smoking like a chimney in the dead of a New England winter.

"Well that was anti climactic," Matilda said.

"Boooo," I said.

Flames licked out at the air from the hatches leading below deck.

"Wish we had some weenies to roast over that barbie," Matilda said.

"We need to get moving." I started rowing.

"Right then, you've got the first shift," Matilda said and leaned back looking out across the open water. "How do you know which direction to head for land? Not much to go by landmark wise."

"Smell," I said. I rowed at an even, but not quite natural pace. I didn't want to go too crazy in front of her, even though she wasn't as put off by anything she had already seen me do. Or had imagined after seeing the blood and body parts all over the deck of the destroyer.

"Hopefully you can tell the difference between the scent of a friendly port and an enemy one," Matilda said.

"I can," I said and kept rowing.

Matilda narrowed her eyes at me. "I guess I should just relax and let you do all the work."

"I'm going to need to go fishing in about an hour," I said. "You can row then if you like."

"I could very well do the fishing while you keep rowing," Matilda said.

"Can you catch a fish with your bare hands?" I asked.

"I doubt it, why?" Matilda said.

"Do you see a fishing pole anywhere in this dingy? Or a spear?" I said.

"No."

"Then I will handle the fishing," I said.

"Of course you can catch a fish with your bare hands out here in the middle of the ocean," Matilda said and shook her head chuckling.

"Or my teeth," I said.

"Why not, makes perfect sense," Matilda said.

We didn't talk again until I was hungry, a few hours later. Matilda had fallen asleep, but woke abruptly when I stopped rowing.

"Are we there yet?" She asked.

"No," I said and stood up. "Hope you like raw tuna."

"What you can't blow fire along with your other talents?" Matilda asked.

"My zippo went down with my ship," I said and dove into the water.

It only took a moment for me to get a hold of a smaller tuna. I had stopped over a school of them and it was very much like shooting fish in a barrel. I tossed it out of the water and it thudded on the bottom of the boat, the sound pulsing though the water right before my head broke the surface.

The fish was still alive and thrashed around inside of the small dingy. Matilda did not look happy. Luckily it was a small fish and couldn't do any damage to the boat, or her.

As I pulled myself into the boat, Matilda stared at me sternly with her arms crossed.

"You're an ignorant ass," she said.

"And you're not going to starve to death," I said. "Hopefully you won't die of dehydration, but I can't promise that. Fresh water is the most elusive of prey out in the middle of the ocean."

"Oh you're hilarious," Matilda said.

I grabbed the fish, put two fingers up in its gills and yanked, gutting it quickly. I tore off a piece of meat and handed it to Matilda.

She took it slowly and said, "Thanks." She bit into the raw fish and swallowed without chewing.

"It would be a shame if you choked to death after everything you've survived so far," I said and tore a chunk of meat out of the fish.

"Maybe," she said as she took another bite, chewing twice this time before forcing herself to swallow.

"How can this be that bad after being held captive by the Japanese?" I asked.

"I'll take torture over this any day," Matilda said and tore another chunk off.

"Why were they torturing you?"

"I'm a spy."

"Not a very good one since you got caught."

"Ever noticed in movies and books how the bad guys always talk about their plans around the main characters in the story when the bad guy thinks they have the upper hand? Same in real life," She said and swallowed the last piece of fish she had whole.

"They discuss their plans in Australian?"

"No, but I speak eight languages," Matilda said. "Including Japanese."

"Maybe you should have focused more heavily on English."

"Will you please start rowing again so this little adventure can end."

I did just that. Night came and Matilda slept most of it. This gave me the opportunity to row much more heavily.

An hour before dawn, I woke her and said, "My turn."

"Fine," Matilda said. She snarled her lips and sighed.

"I only need an hour, you can row in that direction, if you must," I pointed southwest. "Or you can sit quietly. I suggest sitting quietly."

"I'll row," Matilda said as we switched places, the boat rocking a bit. "You better not snore."

"I think that is the least of your worries with those puny little arms of yours," I said and closed my eyes.

An hour later a kick to my feet gently woke me.

"You snore," Matilda said.

I kept my eyes closed and said, "you're still here?"

"Luckily I was holding on every time you farted," Matilda said. "Would have been knocked over board if not for these puny arms."

I opened my eyes and the sun was coming up over the water. It was beautiful. I had seen quite a few of those sunrises the past few months at sea, but that one was the most spectacular I had ever seen. Most likely it was because of the fact that we weren't dead. We had a whole new day ahead of us to try reversing that fortune though.

"What are you staring at?" Matilda looked at the sun rising over the water.

"The sunrise."

"It does that everyday," Matilda said. "And it sets every night."

"Are you dead inside, is that what it is?"

"Not yet, and I would like to keep it that way," Matilda said. "Get rowing. What I know will be useless if we die out here in the middle of the ocean."

"I'm not going to die out here, tried."

"What are you?" Matilda said. "And how did you get on that boat?"

"What?"

"You're not some lowly sailer the Japanese took as a P.O.W. And you're responsible for whatever happened to all of those men. I've heard rumors of soldiers like you."

"I got lucky, just got the upper hand," I said as we switched spots so I could row.

Matilda stared at me for a moment. "I don't know what your government did to you, but I do know that you have the best chance of surviving this. And what I know can't die with me."

"What do you know?"

She sat there for a moment, scrutinizing me as I rowed, then said, "The Japanese have gotten ahold of secret project your government has been working on and they aren't far behind now."

"What project?" I asked.

"It's designation is Manhattan," Matilda said. "I don't know any more than that about it. I do know that the Japanese are working to beat the States to whatever the project is building. The Japanese have two teams working on it in Hiroshima and Nagasaki. The Japanese are finally afraid with Germany surrendering and they're basically a cornered animal now and acting like it."

I didn't say anything after that and Matilda fell asleep again. I ate some more of the fish and hit the oars hard while I had peace and quiet. Luckily we crossed a well traveled fishing lane that was also being used by multiple militaries. Soon enough, I had a gun pointed at me from the port side of a small boat. He was yelling but I was too tired to understand.

I kicked Matilda's feet and said, "Hope one of the languages you butcher is French."

Luckily it was. She actually knew a secret handshake or something, I wasn't really paying attention at that point and the Captain got us to the British Pacific Fleet base at Manus Island.

Matilda got in touch with her superiors and relayed the information she had. She also passed on the relative coordinates of the island where my shipmates were stranded. They were found a few days later. Thinner than they have ever been before, but alive.

A few weeks later the first two atomic bombs were detonated over Hiroshima, then Nagasaki. The world changed faster than it ever has in the days following. I wanted nothing to do with the military ever again with what those weapons meant.

I was dead according to them. I was counted as a casualty of the sinking of my ship because Matilda convinced everyone I was some poor schmuck of a fisherman who got caught in the middle of the battle between my old ship and the Japanese Frigate I scuttled.

I was okay with that.

I found myself wandering around Sydney rather than heading back to the States.

During the last few weeks of the war, I lived above a bar, spending most of my days just drinking and thinking.

Matilda had introduced me to the bartender who owned the building telling him I needed a room.

After a few days of sitting there, the bartender came over with a large Manila envelope rather than a drink and dropped it in front of me.

It was addressed to H.K., the derro/wristy/bogan American, at this bar's address. The letter inside was mostly insults, but there was something else in the package. I held it up and poured the contents into my hand. It was a brass Zippo lighter. There was an inscription that read, 'For when you need to breath fire -M-'.

The day after reading it, I couldn't help myself from writing a letter back to her.

We wrote back and forth for a few months and I knew I was in trouble. Deep down I knew it wasn't going to end well, I knew better but couldn't stop myself. The logic was easy to ignore when that longing sinks its claws in. I looked forward more and more to those letters, to her ball busting and everything she was hiding below the surface.

The war was over and Matilda decided it was time she took her leave of the secret agent game. We set ourselves up on a small piece of land outside of Perth. It was far enough away that I could get into the outback every month for a little me time.

For the first year, it was great. Everything worked between us. The sex was great, the nights out were great even the fights were great.

Until they weren't.

Matilda wanted to know more, she didn't like my vague answers and drank herself stupid and angry more and more. And my adventures every month would be questioned and followed by either the silent treatment or contempt. Sometimes it was contemptuous silence. I have no idea how she pulled that off.

And one night she hit me with the news that she wanted to have a baby. I get it, I wanted children at her age but that just wouldn't be in the cards for her and I. Couldn't tell her the truth, no matter how much she already suspected, and I just didn't have a believable lie at my disposal. So the conversation would always turn into a screaming match.

The last of those conversations ended with Matilda chucking an ashtray aimed at my head. I left for my walkabout a day early with her more pissed than ever. Mostly because she missed.

I figured when I got back from this walkabout I would have to pack & leave or she would cool off while I was away. Or maybe even she would be gone.

But as you have heard time and time again throughout these conversations that's not how situations like that go for me.

When I walked up to the front door of our house, there were muddy boot prints leading up to the door but no boots sitting on the porch. The foot prints were her size and the pattern was the ones we had picked up the month before. The mud was slightly red with chunks of clay and the only reason she would have run into the house wearing them is if she was in a hurry or she was being chased in as she never let shoes be worn into the house.

I could smell her, I knew she was there, but I could also smell the bog where that mud came from. I knew that smell very well as I had spent almost every full moon there for our entire relationship.

When I opened the door and poked my head inside, Matilda buried an ax in my the back of my skull.

No hello, no I saw what you are, no accusations.

Just an axe to the back of my head.

I have to assume that she knew what would happen when she did that and was prepared. She must have seen what I was the night before and she had trapped me in the house long enough to get away.

I was left for the first time vulnerable in a way I had never known. The injury didn't heal perfectly and I had a huge hole in my memory. I didn't know who I was or what I was.

This was very bad, especially for Australia.

I traveled town to town on a killing spree more or less because I wasn't controlling my temper or what I was. I would do something terrible, wake up, and run because I had no idea what happened.

Went this way for months until my past started seeping back in.

Flashes at first.

Then I woke up after a change and started running, naked and covered in blood. I saw a train moving along in the distance kicking up dust and headed straight for it. As I ran the previous night came to me like lightning illuminating a moonless sky. I jumped into an open shipping car and fell to my knees because the memories of the previous few months had finally obliterated whatever was holding them back in my head.

The proverbial dam had burst.

Running mixed the perfect cocktail of endorphins to finish healing not only the severed nerves in the base of my skull, but also sewing the pieces of my heart back into a rough but recognizable shape.

But the river bed is never ready for the flood. The water churns up mud and debris. It tears apart the rivers edge, yanking rocks from the Earth and uprooting trees. I shook and sobbed and my head throbbed as I clenched my eyes and my teeth, digging my finger nails into the wood planks of the train car floor.

After a few moments, I opened my eyes slowly; the light making me squint as though I had stepped into the daylight from the dead of night.

And he was sitting there, his back up against a pile of packing crates tuning his guitar. The man looked surprised but not unhinged at the sight of a naked guy covered in blood jumping into a moving train car.

Australians don't spook easily.

Looking me in the eye, he said, "You alright, mate?"

I looked down at the dry and crackling blood on my skin. "Not really."

"Is that your blood?" He said while reaching into his ruck sack and pulled some clothes out.

I shook my head no.

He held the pants and shirt up for me, "You can have these if you want, they should fit okay."

I took the clothes from him stood up and pulled the pants on first. The blood cracking and flaking off. Then I pulled the shirt on.

"Do you want to sit down?"

I looked out the train car door, then down to the floor.

I leaned my back against the wall next to the door and slid down.

"What do they call ya? I'm Geoff, Geoff Mack."

"Hank, I think."

"You think?"

"Not really sure what's true and whats not up here," I pointed at my head, "with the kinds of stuff that keeps running through my mind."

"Well, Hank, I would say that you've been through something pretty crazy from the looks of ya."

"I think so too."

"Do you like music? That's what I do. I can strum some tunes and it might make ya feel better. Always helps me."

I nodded my head.

Geoff started strumming and I unloaded everything that was going through my head. Tearing bodies apart, drinking marrow from bones I'd broken in half, screams of every age and gender just echoing around the inside of my skull.

Geoff just keep strumming different tunes as I talked. I held nothing back of what I thought I remembered of the past few months.

After a few moments of me not talking anymore Geoff stopped strumming and just laid his arm over the guitar and leaned back into the crates.

"That's some crazy booshit man."

"And then there's a woman. I can't remember her name but her face and her smell, it's like a kick in the head every time I picture her smile or think about breathing her in. Everyone of the faces in my head right now looks like her and smells like her. And I keep tearing them apart."

Geoff leaned forward and strummed the guitar lightly, "From that tale it sounds like you've been everywhere, man. And seen a thing or three."

The next stop was outside of Sydney and I went to hear him play a gig not far from the train station at a small bar, but left before the set was over. I headed into the city to figure out how to get home.

Years later I was back in Australia and tracked down Matilda. She had gotten very sick and I found her in a hospital spending her last few days listening to the radio. That was when I heard the song for the first time,

Geoff Mack's voice telling my story.

I think Matilda might have even guessed the song was about me. Swear I saw a smile on her placid face. That's all I had to go on since she was either giving me the most steadfast silent treatment again or she wasn't able to speak any longer. My money is on the former.

I buried her a few days later under a tree where we used to live together. She had no family, no one besides me.

She should have had more.

Chapter 12

"That was basically a war story," Nick said.

"You can call it whatever you wish," Hank said and tossed another log onto the fire.

"It was a war story," Nick said.

"Now all I can think about is war," Hank said. "Ask one of your dumb questions about something else."

"Tell me about the night your daughter went missing?" Nick asked.

"No," Hank said. The sound of the brass lighter clicked open in Hank's hand and the sound rang in the night air.

"You're going to have to at some point," Nick said.

"No, I don't," Hank said and the clank of the Zippo closing was muffled by his enormous mitt.

"You're not ever going to tell me about the most controversial, life altering moment of your entire story?" Nick asked. "Then why are we having this conversation?"

"Then leave," Hanks said, staring at the fire. His face like stone again.

"Fine, we'll do the stereotypical interview session type question; have you ever met any celebrities?" Nick asked.

"Geoff Mack was a celebrity."

"Fine, have you met any other celebrities?" Nick sighed.

"A few, my favorite by far was Sinatra," Hank said.

Sunshine
Las Vegas - 1956

After I came back to the U.S. from Australia I moved out West again. Everything was booming out there and Vegas offered a unique opportunity being buried in the middle of the desert.

The Southwest was easy to get lost in and was empty in so many directions. I would roam Red Rock or Mt. Charleston for days just for fun, not even during the full moon, but especially then.

I didn't really need a job but life gets boring when you don't do anything constructive. For the first few months I was more or less a professional gambler. I was pretty good, but it wasn't really a good use of my time. Got boring real quick when a bunch of casino goons came up behind me when I was running a table and asked if I wouldn't mind stepping away from the table and speaking to the them in private.

"I would very much mind," I said as I considered my options. I could easily outrun them. I could easily beat them in a fight if they chose to take me by force. But, I was bored and wanted to see what would happen if I went with them. I had heard tales of guys getting their knuckles broken or a .22 to the temple. And neither of those scenarios would really work on me, but could be fun to try. "But, to avoid making you look bad in your work place, I'll take a walk with you."

I took a moment to handle all of my chips, counted thoroughly and stacked neatly.

The goons were mouth breathers.

"Have those winnings added to my house account," I said as I stood up.

"Please follow me," Goon one said and started walking. I rolled my eyes and fell inline behind him. Goon two kept pace behind me. We took a side door down a hallway to a service elevator. We went up to the top floor and walked down another hallway to an office at the end. Inside, the windows looked out over the sparkling lights of Vegas. Everything was gold and burgundy. It gave off a mixed signal on whether it was the kind of place where people were whacked. The burgundy was a good choice , but if any blood got on the gold piping on the couch it would never come out.

There was a desk and very stereotypical mobster type sat behind it. But uglier, like Joe Pesci had been hit by a baseball bat and the bones had set with one eye way higher than the other.

The man looked me in the eye and asked, "Would you please sit down, Mr. Narrow."

"And you would be?" I said as I sat down.

"My name is Mr. Laporta," he said. "I am the head of security to answer your next question."

"So, how may I help you, Mr. Laporta?" I said

"You are an exceptional card player, Mr. Narrow. I've been watching you for quite a while and you don't often walk out of here down," Mr. Laporta said.

"I have been lucky," I said, might as well play along and drag this out as long as possible. It was kind of fun.

"I will cut to the point Mr. Narrow, I know you aren't cheating. You play the long game and know how to work someone who is cheating. I've seen you win over multiple players who were trying to hustle you and the casino. To be exact, you have already helped us find more than a dozen cheats during the time you have spent playing in our casino," Mr. Laporta said.

"You're welcome?" I said not knowing where this was going. "And you've only scratched the surface."

"I would like to offer you a position here, Mr. Narrow, because I feel it is a better use of your talents. Any other measure we might employ would be a waste with a man of your expertise."

"I can honestly say I didn't see that coming," I said.

"Most people who walk into this office don't usually see what's coming next," Mr. Laporta said.

"Now that seems more in character," I said. "What if I pass on your offer?"

"I don' take you as the kind of man who turns down an opportunity to flex his talents," Mr. Laporta said.

"Very well played," I said. "Now I might as well ask what the compensation is for the position?"

Mr. Laporta smiled, picked up and pen and paper from the edge of his desk, wrote down a number, folded the paper in half and slid it across the desk toward me.

I picked it up and read it. "This will be enough to cover a three month contract."

"Excellent," Mr. Laporta said. "You also may find that our organization can offer other benefits along with the fiscal compensation according to your tastes. But we can get to that as we learn more about each other. Would you be free to have dinner with our other department heads tomorrow evening to get acquainted with everyone?"

"I'm sure I can pencil that in," I said.

Mr. Laporta stood up and extended his hand over the desk.

I stood and shook it.

"We can send a car for you tomorrow evening," Mr. Laporta said.

"Excellent," I said and turned toward the door. "I'll show myself out."

"Good evening, Mr. Narrow," Mr. Laporta said as I walked out the door. The two goons were waiting outside the door and followed me to the elevator and down to the main lobby. Another goon was there with a payout from my winnings earlier. I took the cash and left.

*****

The next evening I was picked up at my place out in Boulder City. I preferred being as far away from the city as I could get but near a body of water, and the Hoover Dam and Lake Mead were right there.

Twenty minutes later the car pulled into a long gated drive and drove up to an enormous house on the outskirts of the glittering lights of Vegas. When we came to a stop my door opened and Goon one from the previous night looked into the vehicle.

"This way, Mr. Narrow," Goon one said. I got out and followed him inside.

Inside was all marble and chandeliers, I really wasn't paying much attention to details though.

The goon led me into a room with a small bar in the corner.

As I walked in Mr. Laporta stepped in front of me and said, "Hello Mr. Narrow, thank you for joining us."

"Welcome," I said. It was obvious from the look on his face he had expected me to thank him for the invitation.

"Well then, lets get the introductions out of the way," Mr. Laporta said.

"I'm going to get a drink first," I said and walked past all the men standing between me and the bar without even looking at them. I could feel at least three of the men shift their aggression toward me, probably formulating a hit on me subconsciously if not actively.

Not that there was enough alcohol behind that bar to keep me more than buzzed for a few minutes, I wanted the security a drink gave you. I could actually look at a person over the glass, really scrutinize them without much attention being paid to my eyes while taking a sip.

"What may I get you, sir?" The bartender asked.

"Whiskey on the rocks, make it a double, please," I said. Ice is always a good choice too because it makes that annoying clinking sound in the glass that throws people off even if for a split second.

I grabbed the glass off the bar as soon as the bartender put it down and turned back toward the men in the room. "All right, who is who?"

Mr. Laporta spent the next few minutes introducing me to everyone, telling me their name and supposed position in the casino hierarchy. Then he came to the last man in the room, someone who's voice I recognized but couldn't place.

"And, Mr. Narrow, I presume our last guest needs no introduction," Mr. Laporta said.

"I guess I'll ask myself since he doesn't know who the hell you are either," I said pointing to Mr. Laporta. I held my hand out to the man and his blue eyes lit up.

"Frank, Frank Sinatra," he said and took my hand firmly. "Pleasure to meet you, Mr. Narrow."

"Oh, I've heard your music," I said. "Catchy."

"Ha," Sinatra said. "I like this guy, he's a riot."

Most of the other men laughed at that, which I was a little confused about as I really could have cared less who he was.

During dinner Sinatra sat next to me at the table, and he talked, at great length. That was fine by me as I didn't really care to speak with anyone in particular. Most of the men there were content to listen to him as well, which was also fine by me as I didn't want to know anything more about them.

I have to admit, Sinatra was entertaining, but it was a question he asked me directly that began us on the adventure that would come from that evening.

"What do you think of the phrase lucky at cards unlucky at love?" Sinatra asked looking me right in the eye.

"I'm not really lucky at either," I said.

"Come on, these fella's here were going on and on about how much money you've won at their establishments," Sinatra said and laughed.

"It wasn't luck," I said.

"Not even a little?" he asked stone faced.

"Not even a little," I said.

"Well, you're not the worst looking fella in this room," Sinatra looked at Laporta, "So you've probably charmed your fair share of the fairer sex. Are you married?"

"Once," I said.

"Ended that badly did it?" Sinatra said.

"The end wasn't so bad, but there were quite a few years of terrible preceding it," I said.

"I think you just described every relationship between every man and woman throughout history," Sinatra said then erupted into laughter. Everyone in the room followed suit while I only smiled.

There were a few more small moments of jokes, but mostly it was just Sinatra entertaining as he was famous for. After dessert was served a few of the men politely excused themselves as they had other engagements to attend and I asked for a car to bring me down to the strip.

Sinatra heard my request and chimed in, "I'm headed back there, you can catch a ride with me."

Before I could slink away, Sinatra had his arm around my shoulder. "I've got the T-bird with me tonight. Have you seen all the lights of the Strip from a convertible?"

I didn't answer, not that it would have mattered.

"You're gonna love it," Sinatra said with a huge grin.

His car was waiting outside the door of the mansion where we just had dinner. Part of me just wanted to run and get lost among the cards and the chips and the felt tables of the city, but a small piece of me was curious what might happen with a hammered Frank Sinatra at the wheel.

Sinatra slid into the drivers seat while I stood looking over his head at the light of the city twinkling in the distance.

Sinatra chirped the horn twice, revved the engine, then said, "Hope you don't suffer from vertigo."

I sighed and hopped into the car without opening the door.

"You're a rather nimble fella, aren't you?" Sinatra said as he dropped the car into gear and took off from the mobster's mansion.

I didn't bother putting on my seat belt as he took the winding roads down toward the city at breakneck speeds.

"There's a little get together up on Fremont before an Atomic viewing party, and I think it might be right up your alley," Sinatra said. "If you don't mind a detour before hitting the Strip?"

Most of me thinks I'll hate whatever it is, but I was feeling bored so I said, "I don't have anything else going on this evening."

"You're not a glass half full kinda guy are ya?" Sinatra said.

"No," I said.

"Let's get a few more drinks in ya and a pretty girl on your lap and see if we can change your mind," Sinatra said as he took the turn onto Fremont Street at twice the speed he should have.

Our first stop was The El Cortez. Famously owned and operated by Bugsy Siegel for a few years after the war, but now the Mob influence was light and it was mostly legit.

Mostly.

Some things you still couldn't buy outright even in Vegas corner stores and the Cortez was a favorite place for those who peddled such wares to hang out and relax.

We pulled up in front of the valet and Frank jumped out of the car leaving it running. I opened my door and stepped out slowly.

The valet attendant looked me up and down, then said, "Good to see you tonight Mr. Sinatra." Frank shook the boys hand and I could see a five dollar bill move between them.

"Ready and waiting as always, Nicky," Sinatra said.

"Of course, sir," Nicky nodded as he slid behind the wheel of the car. The engine revved as he massaged it into gear and pulled away to an area where two others were parked behind velvet ropes.

"Seriously, that's only a couple dozen steps away," I said to Frank as we walked in the door to the lobby. "You couldn't have just parked it there yourself?"

"This city loves me because I give them the chance to participate in my life, from guys like Nicky who get to drive my car fifty feet to the guy I buy my smokes from," Sinatra said as he pulled out a pack of unfiltered Camels. He snapped his wrist up, two cigarettes popped up and he offered me one.

I shook my head no and he pulled one out with his lips. His other hand came up with a zippo from his jacket pocket. The click of the lighter opening and him lighting his cigarette was as smooth as it could be. The ember on the end glowed as he inhaled, flicking the lighter closed with a switch of his wrist right before sliding it back into his pocket.

We headed for the elevator, and it opened as though expecting him. He hit the button for the top floor.

"Have you ever seen an A-bomb go off?" Sinatra asked as we were carried up floor by floor.

"No," I said.

"Absolutely beautiful, just breathtaking," Frank said then took a drag off his smoke.

"Everyone in Hiroshima probably thought the same thing," I said.

"That's morbid," he said and shook his head. "We really need to get you a woman. Luckily for you, that shouldn't be too hard with me around."

The elevator doors opened and two casino goons were standing in front of the double doors at the end of the hall. They both smiled as we walked toward them.

"Good evening Mr. Sinatra," The goon on the right, Goon three at this point, said as the other opened the door for us.

Inside the suite was everything I expected. The lights were dimmed and the air was thick with smoke & musky perfumes of all kinds. Everyone had a drink in one hand, a cigarette of some kind in the other and were at least three sheets to the wind.

The room exhaled a unified,"FRANK," as we walked in. A young woman handed Sinatra a rocks glass of whiskey.

Frank took a sip from the glass and said,"Mmhmmhmhmm, just the way I like it. Thanks sweetheart."

The young woman smiled and blushed just enough to keep Frank's attention, "You're welcome Mr. Sinatra."

"Awe, call me Frank, all my friends do," Sinatra said with that grin of his plastered across his face. "And what do they call you, sweetheart?"

"I like the way you call me sweetheart," she said. "But my name is Mary."

"Well, sweetheart, this here is my friend," Frank looked to me and said, "Well, I only know him by Mr. Narrow. What can this young lady and one of here lovely friends call you this evening, Mr. Narrow?"

"Hank," I said.

"Well, nice to meet you, Hank," Mary said. "Let's get you a drink and find one of my friends."

A minute later I was sitting on a sofa across from Sinatra with a whisky on the rocks in my hand.

A few seconds later Mary dropped down onto Franks lap and a young blonde slid onto my lap.

"Hiya, Mr.," she said with a waining southern drawl, "My name is Bobbi, with an i."

"Hank," I said.

"Nice to meet ya Hank," she said. "Have you ever been to an A-bomb Party before? This is my first one. Never seen one go off before, but I hear its spectacular. Just the most amazing thing you'll ever see."

I stopped listening after that. She went on for the next hour without stopping.

Frank and Mary talked for a few moments on the couch, then the two of them made the rounds to different groups of people around the room. He was wooing them all. Then he and Mary disappeared into a back room.

From what I could hear, it was a bedroom.

The suite started emptying out as people made there way to the roof where everyone could drink and party until the bomb was detonated. I could hear music coming from up there, sounded like one of Frank's gang crooning for the party goers.

"You're the strong silent type aren't ya, Hank?" Bobbi said.

"Yup," I said.

"Would you like to go get some fresh air on the roof and find a nice cozy spot to watch the show?" She asked.

That's when I heard the distinct sound of a fist hitting a person's skull. And it came from the back room where Frank and Mary had retired to. I didn't take Frank as the kind to hit a lady, mind you he might have been into something kinky in the opposite direction. Some powerful men like to be dominated. But I doubted it since part of his living came from that face of his.

"Why don't you go ahead and find a nice spot for us and I'll meet you up there," I said.

Now that I was listening I could make out three heartbeats and one of them was slow and steady while the other two were pumping hard with adrenaline.

"Shouldn't be too hard," Bobbi smiled as she ground her bottom into my lap.

"Let's not get ahead of our selves sweetheart. Wouldn't want you to miss out on the rooftop show because we get too caught up with that kind of thinking," I said and motioned for us to stand.

The sound of knuckles on flesh came from the back room.

"Don't go and get lost now," Bobbi said as she looked over her shoulder at me while walking toward the door.

I smiled and watched her leave. I was alone now in the suite. I slowly walked down the hall toward the back room.

The door to the room opened a crack and I saw someone peak out. It wasn't Frank and it wasn't Mary.

They saw me walking toward the door and slammed it shut.

"Seriously," I said. I could hear Frank groan as if waking up groggily.

Then I could hear whispering.

"Guy he came in with is walking toward the room," one guy said.

"Kill him," the other guy said.

Mary must have snuck out at some point. Only three heartbeats in the room and I didn't smell death.

"We should just whack them both and be done with it," guy one said.

"Boss wants us to make him disappear," the second guy said. "So we stick to the plan and get him out to the test site before the bomb goes off."

"I still hate that plan, I don't want to go anywhere near that place," the first guy said. "Those Doom Towns give me flashbacks. Last time looked just like Dresden, you know, before everything happened."

"Stop being such a pansy," the second guy said. "Now go kill that other guy."

"Fine," the first guy grumbled.

The first guy was reaching for the door when I kicked it in. My foot went right through his gut and out the other side. I didn't think he was standing that close to the door.

Totally threw off my groove as I had to shake the dead guy off of my leg and the second guy was able to pull out his pistol and fire point blank into my chest.

Believe you me when I say it is very difficult to control yourself when someone shoots you directly in the heart. My instincts took over and I reacted a little too harshly in retrospect.

"What the fuck?" I heard Frank whisper. He was tied up in the chair, wearing only his skivvies looking at me from the corner of the room. In my left hand was a head, in the other was a body and my leg was through the torso of the other guy.

"I hate you," I said and dropped the head and the body. Then I hopped around the room trying to push and shake the other guy off my leg without tearing him in half.

"Who are these guys?" I asked as I untied Frank.

"They were part of the Giovanni crew, you met their Consiglieri at the party earlier," Frank said as he rubbed his temples. "Holy hell does my head hurt."

"Why would he want you to disappear?" I asked.

"No idea other than money," he said.

"Is there anyone we can call to get us out of here," I asked.

"I... I don't think I can trust anyone," Frank said. "Except you."

"That is a terrible idea," I said. "But we have to clean this up."

"Why?" Frank said as he stood up. "Let's just leave it and send them the message that I'm not a soft target."

"Because I don't want to be involved in this crap," I said. "And you're going to help me."

"But there's blood everywhere," Frank said. "Its all over the carpet, the bed, the curtains and that wall."

I stripped the bed quickly and luckily the blood hadn't soaked through the blanket or sheets. The mattress was clean. "Yank the curtains down and start soaking up the blood from the wall with the pillow cases."

Slowly Frank obliged and got to work. I wrapped the bodies up in the blanket and the sheets, then went to work cutting up the carpet using my claws.

"Where the hell did those come from?" Frank said looking at my hands.

"Don't ask anymore questions until after we are out of this damned hotel," I growled.

Frank kept trying to sop up the blood from around the room as I shredded the carpet.

"Call room service," I said. "Champagne and a fruit platter."

"Seriously, champagne right now?" Frank said.

I growled and went to the bathroom to see if there were any cleaning supplies. I heard the door open and Frank went out to the living room to call down to room service. Luckily under the sink there was a bottle of bleach and some rubber gloves.

When I came out of the bathroom Frank came back into the bedroom. I tossed the rubber gloves at him, then the bottle of bleach. He didn't catch the gloves.

"Start with the bare part of the floor," I said and turned to the wall that Frank had wiped the blood off of. Luckily it had only been some spatter and it hadn't soaked in. I tore off a piece of clean sheet, poured some bleach on it and dabbed at the spots on the wall. Left nothing more than a few wet looking spots.

There was a knock at the door and an announcement, "ROOM SERVICE!"

"I'll get it," I said as Frank looked up from the floor where he was scrubbing the bloody subfloor on his knees.

"Do you have some cash for a tip?" He asked.

It stopped me for a moment, that even in that situation, he wanted to reward the person taking care of him.

"Yes," I said then headed out to the front door of the suite. I reached into my pocket, pulled out my money clip and yanked a ten dollar bill from the fold of bills. Then I looked down at myself. "Damn it."

I switched off all the lights, then opened the door keeping myself hidden behind it.

"I have your champagne and fruit Mr. Sinatra," the young man said.

"Just push the cart inside the door," I said doing my best Frank impression. "Not exactly decent in here."

I held the cash near the door handle and said, "Thanks kid."

"Thank you Mr. Sinatra," the bell hop said as he grabbed the cash. I pulled the cart in a little further and closed the door.

I looked at the cart. It wasn't quite big enough for both the bodies to fit in the compartment underneath, but it was the only one I had and I didn't want to risk having anyone else come up there. I popped open the champagne and drank down the whole bottle. I tossed the fruit platter on the couch as I walked by with the cart to the room.

"I thought it would be bigger," I said as I walked into the room.

"There's no way we're fitting both those bodies on that thing," Frank said.

"Look around the suite and see if there are any overnight bags or a suitcase," I said.

"I can only think of one way of using a suitcase or duffle bag in this situation and I don't think I can help you make that work," Frank said as he left the room.

I stood there listening to him rummage through the closet in the other bedroom as I took measurements of the two dead men by eye. Frank came back a moment later with a suitcase and an over the shoulder leather bag.

"You're in luck," Frank said holding the bags up.

"We're in luck," I said as I picked up one of the bodies and walked into the bathroom.

"How are you going--" Frank started to ask but stopped as I tore the head off the body in the bathtub. He dropped the bags in the doorway as I dropped the head in the sink, neck down, so that the blood could drain.

Frank sat down on the toilet, eyes and mouth stuck wide open staring at the wall.

I went and grabbed the other body. Frank startled when I dropped it in the tub.

"Do you need me to move so you can drain some part of his body in the shitter?" Frank said pointing at the headless body in the tub.

"No, but I do need you to bring the cart in here," I said and yanked the other guys arm off. I thought for a moment and opened the toilet. That was actually a good idea so I stood the arm up in the toilet. Jammed the other arm in as well when it was loose.

When Frank pushed the cart into the room, I had torn the arms off both corpses.

Thankfully the cart had a closed compartment underneath. It would be large enough for me to stuff both torsos inside.

"Go grab the blanket and sheets off the other bed," I told Frank.

He didn't hesitate, just moved smoothly out of the room. I tore the legs off both guys and had the torsos stuffed in the cart before he got back. He walked in as I was stuffing the heads in the leather duffle bag. They fit in there side by side neck up easily; would have made an excellent advertisement for the brand showing how roomie the bag was.

"Frank, still with me?" I asked.

"Yes," he said with a shake in his voice.

"Wrap the legs in the bloody sheets, then the piece of carpet," I said as I opened the suitcase.

He went to work as I finagled the arms into the suitcase. After a few attempts I was able to get the suitcase to close and stay closed when I held it by the handle. It wasn't like those ones with wheels every lazy bastard has these days they pull behind them. Would have made that night way easier if I had one of those back then.

I looked over and Frank was struggling with the legs, they must have been heavier than I figured they were. I helped him get the legs wrapped, then we wrapped the blanket around the carpet. Like a leg burrito. Or whatever the Italian equivalent to a burrito is. Goon manicotti maybe?

I picked up the legs and put them on top of the cart. They seemed to sit sturdily enough leaving the cart handle free to push the stupid thing.

"Luckily your clothes are clean," I said looking at Frank who was still only wearing his underwear. "Get in the shower, scrub the blood off of you and from inside the shower and tub. Dry off and put your clothes back on."

"I think you're in need of a change," Frank said and pointed at my blood soaked pants and shirt. The bullet hole wasn't visible with all the blood.

"I'll figure that out while you shower," I nodded toward the tub.

Over the next ten minutes I took off my clothes, stuffed my pants and jacket into the cart with the dead guys, and cleaned up any drops of blood I found from around the suite. Whomever left those bags here had to at least have a change of clothes so I went through the dresser in the other bedroom and found a pair of pants and a sweater from a guy twelve times my size.

I pulled them on and used my belt to cinch up the pants. Had to be at least a size fifty waste compared to my thirty-four.

I heard Frank get out and let him have a moment to collect himself and get dressed.

When I walked into the room, he burst out laughing.

"Did you rob the fattest guy in the casino for his pants?" He asked as he pulled his jacket on.

"Lucky for us. Big men keep large bags for traveling," I said. "You pick up the suitcase, I'll handle the cart and the duffle bag."

The suitcase gave him a bit of trouble and he groaned, "This thing is heavy as hell."

"You only have get it to the parking garage," I said carefully slipping the duffle bag strap over my shoulder. The strap groaned at the weight inside of it. "Suck it up."

Frank only grimaced as we walked into the living room.

At the door I took one last look around the room. I listened as hard as I could to see where the closest person was to us. There were people on the roof and on the floor below us, but no one else around. I opened the door slowly and pulled the cart out backwards with Frank following. I turned the cart around carefully then headed for the elevator.

I was relieved when I looked at the elevator buttons and one of them read Parking Garage. We couldn't go to the valet off the lobby with these particulate bags.

"My car is at the valet, not the garage," Frank said. He looked down at the bags, then said. "Oh, wait these won't fit in my trunk."

The ride down was excruciatingly slow. I had no idea what or who might be around down there at this time of night. Was there another squad of goons lurking to make sure the job was done?

When the door opened I expected the worst, but my ears put my racing heart at ease as I only counted two heartbeats on the first floor of the garage.

"We're alone," I said and pushed the cart through the doors. I made a B line for the car closest to the exit I saw. Luckily it was a Cadillac with a real big trunk. Even better was that the driver's side door was unlocked.

"I can hot wire it while you load the trunk," Frank said and dropped the suitcase at the back of the Caddy.

"Interesting," I said as I hit the trunk release.

"What do you think was our favorite past-time in Hoboken when I was a kid?" Frank smiled and his eyes shined. I knew his favorite moments from his time boosting cars for joyrides were playing on the other side of those blue eyes.

As I pulled the first torso out of the cart and dropped it in the trunk I heard Frank tear a cluster of wires from under the dash. As I moved the second torso, I heard him strip a wire with his teeth then another. I dropped the blanket wrapped legs in on top as Frank tapped the two exposed wires together and the car turned over. Frank pressed in the gas peddle as he tapped the wires together again and the car roared to life. He revved the engine twice to make his point as I dropped the suitcase and the duffle bag in the trunk.

"I win," Frank said over the top of the car as I closed the trunk.

"I can empty out the trunk and we can switch places and see who is faster?" I said as I walked over to the drivers side.

"Where are you going to take them?" Frank said with a slight laugh as he nodded toward the rear of the car.

"We are going to go get some shovels and bury them in the desert," I said and pushed him into the open door and across the branch seat. I slide in behind the wheel.

"We should bring them out to one of them towns the feds build to test the effects of the bombs," Frank said, his head almost spinning around peering into every shadow

"No." I carefully pulled out of the spot and headed for the garage exit.

"Why not?" Frank asked. "The bombs will vaporize the evidence."

"I don't fuck with radiation."

Frank stared out the windshield, quiet, with nothing to say maybe for the first time in his life.

The streets of Vegas were empty as most people were wherever they were planning to party that evening. I drove the speed limit as I headed toward the only place I could think of getting a couple of shovels from at that time of night, the golf course maintenance shed at The Las Vegas Golf Club.

When I pulled into the access at the back of the golf course Frank said, "We burying them in a sand trap?"

"Only place I can think of that has shovels and no one around," I said as I pulled up to the maintenance shed. "Get two shovels and a pick ax if you see one."

"What?" Frank said. "You go get them."

"You think I'm going to just drive away and take the bodies with me?" I said.

"When you say it like that," Frank said and opened his door. He ran to the shed, opened the door and disappeared into the darkness inside.

I heard him trip over something and then something else clattered to the floor. He was in there maybe four minutes when he emerged with two shovels and an actual axe.

Frank opened the back door and said, "Couldn't find a pick, but figured this could work if we need it," as he tossed the three items on the back seat.

We drove in silence leaving the city behind us as we headed east. I knew a dirt road out that way that wasn't too far where there was no chance of us being disturbed.

"This the spot?" Frank asked when I came to a stop.

I nodded then got out of the car.

Frank didn't move immediately. I gave a him a moment to process what we were about to do as I pulled the bodies out of the trunk.

I heard him take a deep breath then let it out slowly before opening the car door. He grabbed the shovels and the axe. He took two paces from the car dropped a shovel and the axe and dug into the Earth with the shovel he kept ahold of.

I walked over and picked up the other shovel and dug in next to him. I could have dug that hole with my bare hands or even with the shovel in only a few minutes. But I really didn't want to let him off that easy plus I was enjoying his company. I dug much faster than he did and the dirt and sand was pretty easy to move. I had expected it to be much rockier and more packed than it was. When the hole was deep enough, we tossed the bodies in. Frank dragged the suitcase and duffle bag over while I handled the torsos and legs.

When we were done filling it in and spreading the extra dirt around, we patted the Earth down. Suddenly, the sky lit up as though it was the middle of the day. I happened to be looking in that direction and it burned my eyes. I grabbed Frank before he could turn around and look toward the source.

"Don't look directly at it, it'll hurt your eyes," I said.

I watched as the mushroom cloud emerged from the flash of light.

"You can look now," I said and Frank turned around.

We stood there for a moment watching the last bit of light dissipate from the detonation.

Frank took out his smokes and lighter. This time I took him up on his offer. But when he tried to light his cigarette, his hands weren't working very well. I forget sometimes how brutal manual labor can be on mortal hands. I took the lighter from him, got his dart lit, then took care of mine. I held the lighter up and said, "I'm keeping this." Slid it into my pocket.

Frank nodded and said. "I don't think I'm lucky at love or cards either."

"No shit Frank," I said and tossed the shovel I was holding as far as I could huck it.

Chapter 13

"That was my favorite of the stories you've told me so far," Nick said. He reached over and grabbed a beer from the cooler.

"Typical of people in this era," Hank said. "Enamored with celebrities."

"Actually, you painted Sinatra in a very flawed manner," Nick said popping it open. "But what I enjoyed the most was how you helped him even though you had no reason. Or maybe you were a little enamored with his celebrity?"

"I didn't care about his celebrity, but he was extremely likable," Hank said. "Unlike you."

"What does that make you since we spend most of our time with the exact same group of people?" Nick said.

"People enjoy my company a great deal more than yours," Hanks said. "I have an amazing sense of humor and have mastered the art of sarcasm unlike you."

"Really now?" Nick perked up. "Why don't you tell me about the night your daughter went missing."

The lighter in Hank's left hand snapped open and he spun the flint wheel igniting the wick. The flame danced on the end of the case but were just as quickly extinguished when he closed the lid.

Hank pulled another bottle out of the cooler between him and Nick. It was a bottle of hard cider labeled Kelsey Red. He flicked the cap off with his thumb, took a sip then said, "I'll tell you about the time I was a bootlegger in Chicago."

Rotten Apple
Chicago - 1921

The running started small, and mostly because I was already doing it. I had met a John Chapman, better known as Johnny Appleseed, when I was wandering west at some point in the 1830's. Can't really remember what year it was.

John was not really all there, but he was entertaining. What stuck with me though from meeting him was the idea of owning an apple orchard. He had wandered all around Pennsylvania, Indiana and Illinois planting nurseries. After the First World War, I sought out and bought one of those orchards in Illinois.

Because it was already up and running, I threw myself into it. It was simple work and it kept me busy. I didn't really need help considering what I am, so I was alone most of the time, and that got a little tedious. The only real interaction was with the bulk buyers who stopped in once a week as I didn't sell anything directly to the public.

I was producing so much so quickly that I couldn't actually get it out fast enough, so I learned how to make hard cider.

It was so easy it was ridiculous but it broke up the work day. And just like that I had a new product and decided to peddle it myself.

Of course this ended up being a mistake.

The United States was going through a transitional period and the "Dry Movement" was taking hold. Within a year of my new venture, the government passed the 18th Amendment starting Prohibition.

I didn't care and figured out a way to keep my operation up and running.

I was a few hours south of Chicago and I already had outlets in the city. What I didn't expect was the demand that followed or the things people would do to keep it flowing.

Because I didn't have to rely on anyone else's crops to make the cider, I never really worried about how I was going to get hops or barley or any of the other ingredients most distillers and brewers depend on to make their product. I grew all of it on my own land and just looked like a sleepy little apple orchard. So, the demand actually went up for me after Prohibition went into effect.

For the most part, it was easy. The same people who would come purchase the cider before kept coming, at first.

A year in, a few people stopped coming by, and I figured they either got caught or they gave up. I didn't really care either way.

Then someone new showed up, with a couple of friends.

I didn't exactly advertise where I was and I had an understanding with everyone who I did do business with, for apples and the products I made from them, that I was not accepting referrals. The people I did business with had been part of the package when I bought the orchard and a new face was rare and not very welcome even when it stood behind someone who had been buying from day one.

A few new faces all on their own was aggravating to say the least.

I happened to be standing out in front of the main barn, mending one of my baskets when they pulled down the drive. The car came to a stop a few feet away from me and the four men got out in almost perfect unison, as though they had practiced that maneuver many times before.

"Hello friend," the man who had been in the driver seat said. He stood apart from the other three leaning on the car.

"I don't have any friends," I said continuing to weave in a new piece to the basket I was working on.

"Well, you certainly do now. My name is Vincent and have heard great things about your product and that you're very dependable."

"Please leave, Vincent," I said.

Looking to the three guys leaning against the sedan, Vincent said, "Look at this guy not even giving us the courtesy of hearing us out after we drove all this way."

I didn't say another word.

"We have a very lucrative partnership in mind for us," Vincent said.

I walked away.

I opened the barn door and walked inside. I closed the door behind me.

Through a gap in the boards I could see them looking at each other dumb founded as I put away the basket and the mending materials.

Vincent yelled, "Are you kidding me?"

The other three men looked to Vincent for an order.

Vincent stood there for a moment, his lip snarling, then said, "Grab the gas can from the trunk. Burn it all down."

I closed my eyes and sighed.

I took a deep breath, walked back out to the front of the barn and walked right up next to the man opening the trunk.

I may have moved a little faster than any of them could actually see, and when I stopped next to him, he jumped back and yelled, "What the fuck?"

I didn't let him jump far, as I grabbed his right arm and snapped it at the wrist, then snapped it again between the elbow and the shoulder.

He screamed out in pain and the other three men froze.

"How… how did you do that?" Vincent asked.

So I showed him, and the other two men.

They all screamed.

I looked at the four of them on the ground, writhing in pain and said, "If you wish to live, please leave and never come back."

I walked away again.

It took them twenty minutes to regain enough composer to actually get into the car. And I can only guess that Vincent needed help shifting as there was no such thing as an automatic back then.

I went back to the orchard and went about my business for the day.

Problem was people like Vincent didn't like being told no.

A few weeks later or maybe it was a couple of months, I received an invite up to the city by one of the men I had been doing business with. He knew my taste in music and said the singer he had performing in his club would knock my socks off.

I didn't know him well, Jimmy, but he liked to actually come and get the cider himself. He ran the food and drink side of things and liked to take care of the other side of the business: the talent, the patrons and the bribes.

The problem was that I would have the urge to hear some music and they always had a seat for me when I showed up. I never had to wait at the door, or for a drink, and the food was always spectacular.

I drove into the city the next day and checked into The Blackstone hotel.

Chicago was amazing in those days. The energy that flowed through the city because of it's very blatant disregard for what the government was enforcing along with the music that came from the rebellion filled every street, alley, nook and cranny. You could hear it, feel it, taste it, smell it and it opened another sense most didn't want to believe existed or flat our simply didn't understand. Especially to my kind.

I cleaned up after the drive and just walked around the city drinking in the sounds, smells, sights and sensations that filled your senses when you actually pay attention to your senses. And when I was hungry I headed over to Jimmy's club.

I don't even remember the name of the place.

Shit like that is gonna be the death of me; my brain is gonna fry trying to figure out the answer.

When I go to the door, Jimmy was some how there to meet me.

"Henry, so good of you to stop by," Jimmy said as he shook my hand. He always put his left hand over our hands as we shook. I hated that and always forgot he was going to do it. Or maybe I just hoped the look on my face would stop him from doing it.

"Couldn't resist," I said. "I had to see this new singer you brought in."

"I promise you won't be disappointed," Jimmy said and waved me to follow him as he walked inside the building. He lead me to the best table in the club. I never asked him to be so kind, but he always was.

"Don't pull an Irish Exit this time, Hank," Jimmy said through a grin. "I wanna know what you think after the show."

"Maybe," I said as I sat down and a glass of my favorite whiskey was placed on the table.

"See you after the show," Jimmy smiled as he headed back to the door.

I ordered the steak that night and was a bit preoccupied with eating when the dinner music changed over to the main show.

Her voice danced in the air, that's the only way I can describe what was happening.

That feeling, the one where the hair stands up on the back of your neck and you feel like your troubles just float away. It was that times a hundred.

For the short moment of the set, I forgot the pain of what I was, what I had done, I even felt as though I would see my daughter again.

I stood without realizing it and started clapping when she stopped singing. The entire crowd had risen to their feet and were clapping as well.

Then the feeling faded, hard.

So many deaths flashed before my eyes, and I heard the voices of all the people who I had loved including my oldest daughter's.

I heard her laughter and the way she would sing so sweetly to her younger sisters.

I crumpled under the weight of her voice into my chair.

And then I heard her crying, whimpering, sobbing.

The familiar feeling of electricity shooting up my spine and out to my hands made me sit bolt upright.

I took a deep breath, then another, and then another while clenching my fists so fiercely that blood began to drip from them. My pulse was pounding in my ears and my blood was about to boil.

Then I realized what was going on.

I had heard of this happening to a few other's like me.

It was the woman's voice, it wasn't human.

She was a banshee.

I took a deep breath let it out slowly. Then another and let it out even slower.

The pain in my hands subsided.

I looked up at the stage and I could see her staring right back at me.

She smiled, flittered on her heels to her left and headed back stage.

I had never seen a banshee before that day, but I realized after that night that the ones that do try and live in the normal world, often become singers using their powers to manipulate the emotions of their audience. Quite a few of them becoming a little more famous than they planned on and had to fake elaborate deaths or be punished because they pulled the curtain back a little too far on the supernatural world.

Part of me wanted to go meet her, to have her take the pain away again, a bigger part didn't want the inevitable crash to happen again as I only narrowly escaped changing right there in the middle of the club and another part of me hated her for unleashing those memories of my oldest child singing and laughing and crying. The latter sound being one that I do everything in my power to push down, lock away and hopefully one day forget as it reminds me of the biggest failure of my life.

I hated that banshee for making me feel that, to think about how terrible my oldest child's last moments might have been. To make me go over every scenario I had ever conceived of concerning her made my blood start to boil again and I knew I had to leave. I had to find something to distract me.

So, I tossed what I thought the service cost with the exact same amount in a tip on the table and headed for a side door I often used.

My head was now swimming even more than normal and I decided walk the city and just let my senses open up and get over loaded. After an hour of this my mind finally felt clear and in control.

And I was tired in a way I hadn't felt in a decades. Headed back to the hotel walking in that dark that only comes right before dawn and passed out as soon as my head hit the pillow.

I woke up the next day with the sun shining through the open curtains.

I had left the window open and the smell of a fire recently put out lingered in the air.

Fires were pretty common in big cities, and Chicago had seen a few big ones in its time.

My mind jumped back to San Francisco, and I tried to shake it off.

I couldn't and I was hungry so I put on some clothes and headed out to the street.

Subconsciously I followed the smell of the fire in the air and found myself standing near the rubble of where I had dinner the evening before.

The building was burned and only a husk of what it was.

I could smell death in the air.

The fire brigade was still working on the building, making sure every small wisp of smoke was soaked.

A Police Officer was talking to someone over on the other side of the street, but I couldn't see them at first. I caught a few words from him and think he said the fire started around 2 a.m. The officer's back was to me, but then turned to look at the burned out building stepping next to the person he was talking with.

It was the Banshee, her gaze was focused on the sidewalk at her feet and she was crying softly.

My ears perked up as she began to speak.

"He was inside, a beam fell across the office door," she said quietly.

"You mean Jimmy Cassidy?" The Officer asked with a tone of familiarity.

She nodded

My blood began to boil.

The Banshee looked up at the building and I saw her shudder just a bit.

"I tried to move the beam, but I couldn't and no one else was around to help," she said as she caught my eye. "I wasn't strong enough. You need to find who did this."

"What do you mean, ma'am?" The officer said. "Did you see someone start this fire?"

"This wasn't an accident, I just know in my gut it wasn't," she said, her eyes still locked with mine.

She was talking to me.

"Find them and make them pay," she said.

"We'll do everything we can ma'am, but unless you or someone else saw someone starting a fire, I'm not sure there's gonna be much left in the ways of clues with the state of the property," the officer said and waved his hand over the scene in front of them dismissively.

"I'm confident you will find them. I'm sorry I couldn't do more and I'm sorry if I brought anything up that might have bothered you," the Banshee said.

"What do you mean by bothered me?" The officer said.

"Nothing, its been , I need to go home," she said, nodded to me just enough for me to notice and walked away from the officer.

I turned my attention back to the building and closed my eyes. I breathed in through my nose and put every ounce of my energy into reading what I sensed.

It wasn't hard to pick out the scent of Jimmy from everything else, it was definitely his and it was mixed with the smell of death and burning.

I wasn't surprised by that or the fact that I was upset at his loss even though I hadn't felt that about anyone in a very long time. I was also a little relieved that it became my singular focus, pushing every other thought out of my mind.

What surprised me was the smell of gasoline mixed with the smell of someone I had recently had dealings with - Vincent.

I rolled over the information for moment and realized what had happened.

I was the actual target.

The target and the timing were too much of a coincidence. I was there and must have missed being followed because of the city and how it made me feel. Couple that with the Banshee and me slipping out a side door, and I missed it.

Because of me.

Vincent and those pieces of trash of his were trying to burn me alive in that building.

I was now very, very, very angry.

I should have let it go.

I knew nothing good would come from me giving a shit.

But I couldn't let it go.

I couldn't shake the feeling of needing to repay the courtesy Jimmy and Cassidy always showed me.

As I've talked about before, no matter how much I say I want solitude, I just can't help reaching out and being a part of the human world for just a short time. And Jimmy helped me do that in small, perfect doses with his club.

These mobsters took that from me.

Luckily for me I knew what Vincent and his men looked like but also what they smelled like.

Took me all of an hour to track them to a small Italian joint on Ashland Avenue just north of Division Street.

I stood on the corner opposite where I could see them through the window.

My gut reaction was to walk in there, tear them apart, paint the walls with their insides and then burn the place to the ground.

But my other senses prevailed as I could hear an old lady cooking in one of the apartments right above the restaurant. And on the top floor a woman was hanging laundry out the window over the alley with two toddlers at her feet.

I took a deep breath and closed my eyes.

I knew there was a better way.

At the moment my conscience was pretty clear on what Vincent deserved, and my imagination was ramping up. But the others in the building didn't deserve to hear me or see me or stumble upon what I wanted to do to Vincent and his men. Plus the police and the FBI were already very interested and concerned with anything out of the ordinary happening in Chicago.

I took another breath and I knew what I would do.

I would give them what they wanted, full access to my cider, my land, whatever they wished.

On the next full moon.

*****

I had my lawyer reach out to Vincent and set up a meeting. My lawyer relayed the terms and the prices I was willing to work with them at.

Twenty percent below what I was selling at before their visit.

He wanted me to be scared, after what he did to Jimmy and Cassidy, but compliant rather than dead. They could make more money from having me make the product cheap and they certainly didn't want to make it themselves. Guys like them never wanted to actually do the work, they just wanted to take from those who could make something.

This is what he expected.

He was scared too.

When Vincent showed up at my orchard, he had ten men with him, half of them carrying Tommy Guns, along with his truck.

It was the late fall and the sun was already low in the afternoon sky.

The sunset would be beautiful that day, I just knew it, and the air was crisp with that mix of decaying leaves and apples that only come as the trees are turning red and yellow and orange.

I wasn't out front to greet them like they were expecting.

I left a crate full of hard cider in front of main barn off the driveway.

"Where the hell is this guy?" Vincent said looking around at the group

119

of men with him.

Most of them shrugged, some shook their heads, two of them pointed their chins at the orchard.

"Spread out," Vincent yelled. "FIND HIM!"

The men did as they were told and moved quickly into the orchard.

I let them wander for a half hour before I grabbed the first one.

I made sure the others heard his scream.

But only one.

As I expected the other men all raced toward the sound of the scream. What they found when they got there was a headless body and the trees dripping with blood.

I'll be honest, I don't remember much after that as I let the moon take hold.

When I woke up the next day my property was riddled with spent bullet casings. Took me forever to clean them all up.

None of Vincent's men survived as expected. Most of them were in pieces, and I never found all of the body parts but it didn't matter. As long as I buried most of them deep on my property no one was going to find anything as scavengers and carrion would take care of the scraps.

I never found anything of Vincent.

He was definitely dead.

I could smell his death on the air.

From everything I've told you so far, his final resting place would likely be my out house.

I kept up the business for a year after that, but everything was getting worse in Chicago. Rumors of Vincent and his crew disappearing helped keep people at bay from me but those fears faded and men I had no interest in dealing with began showing up to make me offers. I refused of course and decided to use the government to cut off my distribution. I had my lawyer report my activities to the authorities and made sure the raid went down when someone I didn't want on my property was taking advantage of my barn being open with hundreds of gallons of cider sitting there like candy in a baby's hand. It was shame too, because that years harvest was absolutely amazing.

I walked away from it with plans in place for my lawyer to purchase the land after the government seizure under a dummy corporation then lease the property to the descendants of one of my brothers. A distant nephew that had visited what he thought was a cousin had fallen in love with the idea of running an orchard.

I loved that property and didn't want it to ever be developed or owned by some Monsanto type farming conglomerate. Who better to lease it to on the cheap than family.

They still use one of the steam powered presses that I did back then.

Chapter 14

"Gonna have to order a few more cases from them," Hank said dropping the bottle he had been drinking among the other empties next to the fire. "That was the last case they sent some my way."

"What the hell! One of your brothers descendants?" Nick cocked an eyebrow toward Hank. "How many siblings did you have?"

"I was born on a farm in the 17th century, of course I had siblings," Hank said.

"What were all of their names?"

"Marty, Natalie, Joseph, Johanna then me, Elizabeth, Michael, John and William," Hank said counting on his fingers.

"I find it hard to believe you had siblings," Nick said. "I can't picture them allowing you to survive cause you must of been an annoying child."

"I'm like this because of them," Hank said. "Johanna was the worst, she tormented me everyday. Made me do half of her chores as soon as my hands were big enough to do them."

"So, which brother's descendants work that orchard out in Illinois?" Nick asked.

"Joseph," Hank said.

"What happened to your siblings?" Nick asked.

"They died," Hank said. He grabbed another beer and twisted the cap off.

"That would be the logical course of events except for the fact that I'm talking to you, a 300 year old Werepig," Nick said. "I meant more specifically, what happened with their lives, did they ever find out about you, did they all have kids or any other facts about their lives you can share?"

"They all had kids." Hank took a big swig from the bottle. "No idea what most of their lives were like as I lost touch with them as they married and moved away. Except for Joseph."

Brother
Kelsey Town - 1681

"Henry," Joseph said as he opened the chicken coop. "You have to learn how to slaughter and clean a chicken. You're not a baby any more."

I was standing behind him.

"Grab one and bring it to the stump over there," Joseph pointed to a blood stained stump with a hatchet buried in the wood.

"I don't want to Joe," I said. I was seven at that point I think.

"You don't have a choice Henry," Joe said. He always called me Henry, never Hank. I only put that together after he died.

My shoulders slumped as I walked into the coop past my brother as he held the door.

I reached for one of the chickens. She was an older hen.

"Not that one, Henry," Joe said. "One of the younger ones. Older chickens aren't good for eating, tougher meat."

Joseph had his own motivations for having his seven year old brother grab a young, easily spooked chicken.

The one I picked was particularly motivated not to be held and I struggled to hold it down on the chopping block.

My brother yanked the hatchet out of the stump and held the handle toward me. "Take it," he said.

I took the hatchet and my arm fell to my side under the weight.

I grabbed it with both hands to lift it but I let go of the chicken.

The chicken wasn't as stupid as it looked, and took off.

My brother started laughing then said, "What are you standing around for, catch her!"

I dropped the hatchet and darted after the chicken. Every time I reached out to grab her, she took a b-line at 90 degrees to the right or the left.

My brother just laughed and laughed and laughed.

This happened every day, for what felt like decades but was only a few weeks, until I was finally strong enough to hold the hatchet and the chicken at the same time. By that point I was so annoyed with how difficult carrying out that task was and hated the chickens for making it so hard that I didn't even care that I was killing it.

I held the hen down on the stump, my little fingers buried in the feathers at the base of her neck, dug into her skin. She squirmed and writhed and fought against my small hand. But I leaned my body weight into her to keep her in place. She made it kind of easy because she was craning her neck out trying to get leverage with her beak in the stump as her feet kicked and ran and clawed for traction on anything. I knew there was no way I could miss and I brought the hatchet up over my head, and then back down with all of my strength.

Of course I let go as soon as the ax buried into the stump. The little head tumbled into the dirt followed by a spurt of blood from the neck.

I had seen a chicken slaughtered before, but as the body slipped to the dirt and the chicken's feet caught the ground, my breath got caught in my throat. The birds little legs scrambled through the dirt in front of the barn leaving its head behind. The animal's body kind of bounced around on top of the legs with blood spurting out a little less with every step it took.

Right then, I felt terrible. All the anger I had built up toward the chickens, for making it so hard to catch and keep a hold of, vanished. I had looked away from the running body to the chicken's head where the eyes sat open and vacant. The hatchet slipped out of my hand and I walked in the direction the hen's body was heading. It stumbled and fell into a patch of grass where it twitched as I took one agonizing step after another toward it until I stood over it.

My brother watched the whole time, not saying a word, not telling me what to do, but giving me gentle corrections as needed.

I reached down and picked up the animal's body, brought it to the back porch and prepared her for dinner by plucking out all of the feathers. It took much longer for me than when I helped Joseph do it. When I was done I buried her head under a tree near the barn.

Thinking on it now, I kept up that tradition with the chickens the rest of my childhood. Looking back on everything I've told you so far it stuck with me long after.

Joseph was in charge of most of my education on our farm it seemed. Either because he was forced to by our father or because he enjoyed teasing me. He was a very good teacher so I always suspected that he volunteered for the job.

From the time I learned to slaughter and prepare the chicken he was beside me. That is until I was fifteen and he decided to join the New England Militia as a Ranger to fight in King William's war in 1689 with New France and the Wabanaki Confederacy. The Wabanaki were a group tribes that called modern day Maine and Nova Scotia home.

My father was a violent man even by 17th Century standards. This was never more apparent than when one of his children did something against his wishes.

"I'm going to go protect what we have built here, father," Joseph said. He stood behind our dad who was kneeling down and tending the fire in our living room.

"No one is threatening our lands, Joseph," my father said as he stoked the fire.

"I didn't mean only what our family has built," Joseph said.

My father was a large, strong man, but my brother had taken after him in that respect and from where he was standing, Joseph knew he had the advantage if our father decided to lunge at him.

The iron poker my father had been stoking the fire with was just sitting in the hot coals under the new logs that had been added a few minutes before.

"I have already signed my name and I cannot go back on that," Joseph said, standing firm.

My father stared into the fire for a moment, took a breathe, then spun around with the red hot fire iron.

Joseph had figured on our father trying to strike him with a fist, but not with the iron fire poker.

Our old man knew my brother was ready for a beating, even that he might be able to win these days. But Joseph couldn't dodge the fire iron. It struck him across his left cheek, and sizzled as it met his skin and hair.

To the old man's surprise, Joseph only fell to one knee.

Father yanked the iron rod back, tearing it from the flesh that sounded like a sausage being romped from a sizzling pan.

Bringing the iron poker up again for another strike, Joseph rose to his feet and caught my fathers arm as he brought it down.

My father was flipped over my brother's back as Joseph stepped and turned his hips into my old man's gut while yanking down on his arm.

The fire stoker clattered away as my father went through the table in the center of the room. My father had a blank expression on his face the whole time.

Joseph looked down at our father, then to me.

"Always work hard, Henry," Joseph said. He smiled then turned and walked out the front doo.

My father looked toward the door resting on his elbows and stomach and muttered to himself, "You may just survive this war, boy."

My father looked over to me, then pointed at the iron poker, then to the fire place.

I grabbed the fire iron and placed in the holder where it belonged.

We didn't say anything else and I went about my chores for the day, alone.

*****

It was four years later that I saw Joseph again. Our father had died shortly before my brother returned; we weren't even sure if Joseph was alive and had no way of getting him word of our father's death.

I found him standing over our father's grave on my nineteenth birthday after one of our neighbors mentioned to our mother that a man who looked like Joseph asked to be shown where the Kelsey plot was in the cemetery.

"Hello Henry," Joseph said as I walked up and stood next to him looking down at the graves in the Kelsey family plot.

I looked over at him, the left side of his face which still bore the scar from the day I last saw him and said, "Hello Joseph."

"You've grown quite a bit," he said. "I think you may be the biggest Kelsey there has ever been."

By that point I stood at least half a foot taller than he or my father had.

"Glad to see you're still whole, brother," I said.

Joseph held up his right hand. His pinky was missing and half his ring finger.

I didn't say anything but the look on my face gave away my curiosity.

"Story for another time," he said. "Which one is his?"

"The one with his name on it," I said and pointed at it. I said with the same curiosity plastered across my face.

"Part of that story for another time, Henry." Looking down at the grave, Joseph asked, "Will you walk with me to see mother?"

"Of course," I said and we headed back to the house.

"Where have you been, Joseph?" I asked as we headed off the main road onto a deer path that was a shorter route to our farm.

"So many places," Joseph said.

"And one of those places couldn't have been home, to visit?" I said.

"There were so many battles to fight, Henry," Joseph said. "So many more to come."

"You're not going away to fight again are you?" I asked as we walked along the trail with the trees full of green around us.

"No, my time at war is over," he said looking down at the ground.

"Good," I said. "I don't want you to leave again."

My brother stopped and took me by the shoulders. He looked into my eyes and said, "I didn't say I was staying here, Henry. I need you to know that first."

"What are you talking about?" I said. "Where else would you go?"

Letting go of my shoulders, my brother started walking again, "I have a wife now, Henry, and a child on the way. You're going to be an uncle. But she and I have decided to take over her father's farm as her brothers were both killed in the wars."

I followed behind him slowly at first. Then I felt a sense of wonder I hadn't felt in a while. "Wait, you're going to be a dad? Is she here with you? What's her name? Where is she from?"

"Slow down," he said. "No, she could not make the journey with me as she was not really up for it. Here name is Katherine and her, I mean our farm is in a little village called Longmeadow, Massachusetts. It's close enough that you can come visit once the baby is born."

"Can I come live with you?" I asked.

"I think mother would have a problem with that as Marty and I have already spoken and we have agreed that you are to inherit our father's land," Joseph said.

"Wait, what?" I said. "You went and saw Marty before coming to see mother or me?"

"It was on the way here, Henry. He and his oldest son will be here by dinner time this evening."

"What if I don't want to stay here? What if I want to go out to the frontier or become a sailor?"

"Do you want to do that, Henry?" Joseph asked. "Is there anything you want to do other than run this farm?"

"No, but..." I started not knowing what I wanted to say.

"We aren't suggesting this to burden you, we are doing this because Marty and I both have land of our own and want the land to stay in our family. You are next in line, Henry. John, William and Michael are too young to have them take over yet with father gone."

I didn't know what else to say. I was happy that they thought I was responsible enough to handle the farm, but I was jealous of Joseph for having gone off on all these adventures I had concocted in my head from the stories that people told of the war.

I don't actually remember what my mother said when she saw Joseph. I only recall the crying and blubbering over him. We laid her to rest next to my father the next year.

And I don't remember dinner at all that evening but plans were sorted out and made concerning the Kelsey Farm and my future. At least what little I had ahead of me as a man.

Joseph stayed for a few days, and he confessed to me that he had to give up soldiering after taking an axe to his skull. It had almost killed him, and left him unable to read any longer. And he found himself confused with new activities, and it was a handicap that he could not afford as a soldier. The only reason it hadn't killed him was he was able to slow the assailants blow with his hand sacrificing a few fingers.

Luckily his hair covered the scar.

He and his wife had four children before she was taken by a fever. He was a happy father, but it was obvious what she meant to him after she was gone as he did not marry again. Which was odd for that time.

We visited each other as often as we could, but after what happened to me, that changed. When I left my family, I went to see Joseph and told him the short version of my misfortune and that I was not welcome at home. He seemed to understand more than he was letting on though as I had left out what I had become.

Once I realized age was not affecting me the same as it was others, I stopped visiting and only wrote to him from my travels. Or just from Nantucket. Luckily one of my nieces stayed close by to him and was gracious enough too read to him and take dictation for letters to me.

But when he was sixty-seven, I received word from my niece that she did not think her father was going to be with us in this world much longer.

I made the choice to go see him.

It took no time at all for me to get there with what I am. But I waited until he was alone, late at night to go see him.

Sneaking into the house where he lived with his daughter and son-in-law, I opened his door to find him awake sitting up in his bed with a candle burning on the nightstand.

A smile stretched across his slack face.

I was looking at the old man I would never have the chance to become.

"Hello Henry," Joseph said quietly.

"Hello Joseph," I said. "You look terrible."

"You don't," he whispered with labored breath. "I knew that you wouldn't."

I didn't say anything but the look on my face gave away my curiosity.

"While I was away at war, we saw and heard things, Henry," Joseph said with in short breaths, "that couldn't be explained in a world under a Christian God and confirmed all those ghost stories that we heard whispered growing up. After what happened between you and that witch, I know what you were."

Joseph laughed quietly and it quickly turned into a cough and his entire body shook and shuddered. After it passed he gasped for air in short, shallow, painful breaths.

"You're dying, brother," I said.

"I know," he said. "Don't know how I lasted this long with all of the things I have done."

"Can I get you anything?" I asked.

"No, but will you sit here with me until… until I pass?" He asked. "I know it will be tonight."

I nodded and pulled a chair close to the bed.

I held his hand as he slipped off in his sleep.

On the nightstand, behind the nub of a candle was a letter with my name on it. It was written in my nieces elegant handwriting. I picked it up and headed out to sit on the east bank of the Connecticut River as the sun rose.

I read the letter. It was the story of how he lost his fingers, a Penobscot Medicine Woman, and what she did to save his life that left him able to see the other side of the curtain, including what I was. He always held onto a sadness that I stopped going to see him, but understood that I wasn't able to tell him everything. He understood my need to keep what I was secret, to keep it buried as best I could. He knew it was the only way I could handle what had happened to me.

I have the letter sealed in polyurethane in a safe deposit box. I'll show it to you if you wish Nick for this… this… project we are working on.

I haven't looked at it in years, it would be good to read it again, and it might give you a clearer picture of my brother.

I wish I had told him what I was, even after all these years. The letter let me know that he would have at least been willing to listen, even if he couldn't understand everything. Being what I am and from the time I am from makes it so easy to fall into the trap of not talking about what's going on up in my head, to bury it down as far as possible, to act and wish and convince myself I don't feel a god damn thing. Sacrificing who I am always seems like a worthy offering to control what I am.

When they buried Joseph I kept my hat low over my face and my eyes on the casket while standing in the back of the crowd.

My dear, dear, dear little brother,

You will never truly appreciate how much joy I got out of saying that while looking up at you all these years. When I came back from the war and you towered over me, I was mixed with pride and envy and admiration at the possibilities before you.

But it never equaled the amount of sadness I had not seeing you for all these years. I knew why you stayed away though. I'll never claim to understand what it is you became, but I knew you were no longer whole after the loss of my niece, your sweet, kind, wonderful daughter. Not just the darkness that came with her absence, but what I can only describe as the second skin that covered you as if you were wearing an animal hide cloak with the head as a cowl.

I never thought less of you for that, quite the contrary. I think of you as the strongest person I have ever known. Shouldering this, this, this curse all alone. I couldn't fathom the toll it has taken on you. I wish you would have talked to me though, I wish that you would have let me help you. But I understand why you didn't. And I'm sorry I never found a way to tell you what I knew, but I didn't know how to explain what I can see. Fear also played a significant role as I was never sure if what I was seeing was real, a hallucination, a result of my injuries in the war or just plain witchcraft. The Penobscot Medicine Woman who nursed me back to health used magic & medicine to bring me back to this world. She didn't speak English and my terrible understanding of her tongue left me with no real explanation of what I now see in the world, and in you, that has no logical explanation.

I hope that I see you again little brother, in this world, but think that it won't be until the next we get to speak again. I know I won't be here much longer, as it is my time and God is calling me home. Its an interesting sensation, such as when one can feel the horses gallop through the ground before hearing or seeing the stampede.

I have one request, please keep writing to my Anna, she has loved taking my letters and reading yours to me all these years. I hope that part of why she loved doing this was because of sharing it with me, but I know she loves writing and hearing from you.

I hope that you find a way to rest one day and will miss you more than I can convey with just mortal words.

Your Big Brother,
Joseph

Chapter 15

"I wish I could have had a brother," Nick said looking up at the stars.

"Wish in one hand, shit in the other. Guess which one fills up faster." Hank said.

"Still a stupid saying even after thirty years of hearing you repeat it," Nick said.

"It's true," Hank said. He grabbed another log and dropped it on the fire.

"I still would have enjoyed having a brother."

"I think you would have been a terrible sibling."

"Why the hell would you say that?" Nick said and turned full his attention to Hank.

"You're super wrapped up in yourself, you were bred to be an only child."

"That is the dumbest thing I have ever heard."

"The dumbest thing you have ever heard was yes, when Mina accepted your proposal."

"Tell her that and see how she reacts," Nick said and leaned back on the hammock turning his gaze back to the night sky.

"I tell her that pretty much every time I see her. For someone that is supposed to be super observant you miss a lot."

"Maybe I just don't listen to you cause you don't add anything to a conversation," Nick said lacing his fingers behind his head.

"Does that mean you haven't been listening at all tonight?" Hank asked.

"At times I wish I hadn't."

"Then give me another prompt so we can get on with this."

"Let's just get it over with. Tell me about the night your daughter went missing?"

The Zippo clicked open in Hank's left hand.

"No." The lighter clacked closed.

"Come on, this is really testing my patience."

"Try not knowing something for over three hundred years."

"That's not fair, I won't have the chance to live that long."

"You don't want that chance."

"You're right."

"I know I am."

"Don't let that go to your head."

"Give another prompt so I can think of something else?"

"Fine, who is your favorite band or singer or whatever?"

"Alice In Chains."

"I wasn't expecting that."

"What were you expecting?"

"A classical composer or the guy in Australia."

"Geoff Mack," Hank said. "Why would you think that?"

"He wrote a song about you, so I figured you'd be all about him."

"I'm not that vain."

"Seriously?"

"Seriously what?"

"You're trying to tell me you're not one of the most narcissistic creatures on this planet?"

"I don't care what I look like or what people think about me."

"Really? You're arrogant, have no regard for others feelings, you can't handle even the slightest bit of criticism, and your sense of entitlement is mind boggling. And asking someone to compile your biography is a pretty narcissistic request."

"Again I need to point out that you keep talking to me and asking me questions," Hank said. "And the number one reason I asked you to sit and go over this with me is I need you to hear all of this. Well, as much of it as I can remember."

"Fine, do you remember a story about Alice In Chains you want to share?"

"Well, actually, yeah."

Bleed The Freak
Seattle - 1990

I was out in Seattle for business.

This was when you and Mina were off at college for some reason and Penny was doing her shapeshifting thing with Mina's cousins.

Ether way, I was in Washington during the fall of 1990 looking into a new investment I was interested in and I had never been out there. Killed two birds with one stone.

The first day in the city, I was sitting at a coffee shop after having lunch, just watching the crowds in Pike Place Market.

There was a paper sitting on the table when I sat down, half crumpled, and stained a bit from where someone had already spilt coffee on it. I happened to look down at it and saw a headline that went something like 'Uptick In Homeless Deaths Around City.'

It was vague but morbid and peaked my interest, so I unfolded the paper. Sadly, it was a short article. A body had been found in an area of the city called The Jungle. It was the fourth death this month. The police department's official stance leaned toward drug abuse and exposure.

That didn't really sit well with me. Having spent time on the streets wandering and pan handling, I know that most folks who end up drifting like that are strong, hardy. Just not usually in the way that keeps them employed or able to handle societal norms.

Drugs can account for some of them being on the streets and even dying there, but my gut was telling me something else. I didn't know what but I knew I wanted to see this place called The Jungle.

I grabbed the paper and headed back to where I was staying.

Back at my hotel room, I grabbed my camera and went over to the concierge. Tourists can ask anything and be taken seriously.

"How are you doing today sir?" The concierge said then pointed to my camera. "Heading out to take some pictures of the city?"

"Yeah," I said and put the paper down on the counter. I pointed to the article about the dead vagrants. "Where is this place?"

The concierge scanned the article quickly. "I'm not sure you want to head there, sir. Its a shame the stories that have been swirling around the city about that place and the parks. I can direct you to a dozen better sites than what you're asking."

"I'll end up seeing all the cliche spots at some point on this visit." I held up the camera and said, "Looking to see something less polished through this lens."

"Well, its The Jungle then I guess," the concierge said then pulled a map from under the counter. "I'll show you where that is on here."

"Thanks, and what stories are swirling around the city?" I asked as he pointed to the map.

"We're here and The Jungle is over here running along I5. Fifteen minute cab ride. And people are saying there's more going on down there than some desperate folks taking self medication too far."

"Like?"

"The management doesn't really like us going into details or repeating rumors. We're only supposed to suggest areas to avoid."

"Come on," I said. "It'll stay between you and me."

The concierge looked around the room, then leaned closer over the counter and said quietly, "People are saying there's a serial killer going after drug addicts and sinners."

"Possibility," I said and grabbed the map. As I walked away I said, "Thank you for your help."

"You're welcome," the concierge said.

I went back to my room and ditched my camera then walked over to the area referred to as The Jungle. Took it quickly, but slow enough for pedestrians to just think I was in a hurry. In another city this may have been a manicured park. But I think Seattle didn't care much for it. They built parts of the highway right over it, leaving it to fester.

I walked the perimeter, making note that to the east were residential neighborhoods and to the west were commercial properties. Mostly warehouses and industrial buildings. Running up the center was an actual forest of maple trees and blackberry brambles.

I headed into the Jungle on the east side from an area labeled Beacon Hill on the map. No one who went west seemed to be able to come up with their own names for places. Always something recycled from where they came from or wanted to emulate.

The division between the residential area and The Jungle was immediate. The smell, the feel of the air and the sounds were stale and stagnate and pungent. Death and sickness were stuck in my nose but not as bad as I have encountered in the past or some other countries. That is one good thing about our country, as long as you aren't picky even a hobo can eat well enough.

The few people I saw quickly scurried away from me. I wasn't here to stress people out, but I did need to find someone who might talk, even just a little bit about what's been going on there.

I was only wandering around inside The Jungle for about a half hour when I found an area marked off by police tape. There were a couple of tents, piles of trash and a dozen or so bicycles leaned up against trees.

It also smelled like blood.

Inside the marked off area, I looked inside of one of the tents as it was open. Blood covered the inside walls and ceiling.

Drug addicts have been known to nick an artery and bleed all over the place, but there was another smell lingering near the tents that confirmed the feeling in my gut.

Lavender.

It's not out of the ordinary for there to be a couple of blood sucking mosquitos in a city, but its another for one to be making the newspapers. Even if it was a vague article buried in the middle of the paper.

I hate vampires.

And this one was a sloppy piece of greedy trash.

As you know they don't need to feed every night, or even every week, unless they are young.

Hunting wasn't exactly what I wanted to be doing on that trip, but my other option was to hope the other filthy blood suckers who lived in the city would take care of it.

But they never do.

They seem to like the chaos their young create. Only getting involved if their existence is threatened directly or another group of supernatural creatures confronts them about it.

I was all alone. I didn't know anyone in Seattle that could help me or point me in the right direction. I had been hoping to find a nice jazz club or something that night. But it seemed my dance card was now full.

I closed my eyes and took a deep breath through my nose.

In a big city now a days its almost impossible to track something by scent because of all the exhaust from cars and trucks but I picked up just enough to work with and made my way north. It was late in the day now and it was slow going tracking through the brambles and trash in The Jungle.

The mosquito wasn't in The Jungle anymore though. I followed the scent back into the city but lost it after a few blocks.

The sun was dipping down in the sky over Elliott Bay and I was getting hungry.

I found a deli and got a sandwich.

It wasn't enough so I bought two more.

I hit that shop anytime I find myself in Seattle.

I decided to keep walking while eating knowing there was no practical way for me to keep hunting that mosquito. Those things aren't good at much, but hiding is one of them.

As I was walking, near an intersection, some kid held out a flyer flicking it with his fingers like he took a class on how to do that.

"Do you like music?" The kid said as I walked by. He had a safety pin though his eyebrow.

"No," I said.

"That was a trick question man, everyone likes music," the kid said and held the flyer out for me. His cutoff gloves had studs sticking out the back.

It hit me slow, like when someone steps in dog shit but didn't clean it off well enough.

"Do they sell whiskey at that place?" I stopped and asked the kid.

He held the flyer out, closer to my face. The smell of blood laced with lavender was unmistakable, and it was the same as the blood painting the inside of that tent in The Jungle.

"Yeah, they sell whiskey," the kid said still holding out the flyer.

"Does the club pay you to hand out these flyers?" I asked as I took it.

"Yeah, why?" The kid said.

"Someone from there gives them to you?" I asked.

"Yeah," the kid said. "The flyer gets you a discount at the door."

I took a deep breath, trying to learn more, but couldn't get anything else from the flyer. The kid was telling the truth though.

Someone who had touched that bum from the Jungle's blood worked at that club. Then touched these flyers. But it wasn't this kid.

"Do they print their own flyers?" I asked.

"How the hell would I know, man" the kid said.

"How far is this place from here?"

"Ten minute cab ride," the kid said.

"And by foot?"

"You don't want to walk that. Not at night."

"Yes I do," I said.

"Twenty minutes that way," the kid pointed north. "Nothing goes straight there so you'll have to zig zag along the highway. It's right near the Denny Way Bridge over the 5 on Eastlake Avenue. It's literally right next to an off ramp."

I looked at the flyer, the place was called the Off Ramp Cafe.

"Thanks," I said and headed in the direction he pointed.

Luckily for the kid I was out of his hair and a group of young punks who looked just like him were heading his way.

The walk took about what the kid said.

The club was a rat hole and the music coming from inside was loud. Louder than I wanted to deal with but I could also smell the dead hobo's blood.

Whatever killed him had been in that building.

At the front door I handed the doorman the flyer.

"Five bucks with this, man," he said.

I handed him a ten. "Do you guys print those flyers here?"

"Yeah," the bouncer said and handed me a five dollar bill back. "One of the guys in the office makes 'em all."

I nodded. "He around tonight?"

"Maybe, not sure," he said and turned to the person that walked up behind me.

I headed inside.

The music was loud, morose and chunky rock & roll.

At first I wanted to hate it.

But I could feel it, I could smell it, in the air; the guys in the band were meant to be playing together on the stage and there was an electricity like I had felt only a few times in the past.

At the bar, I asked for a whiskey.

The bartender plopped my glass down on the bar and yelled, "FIVE BUCKS!"

I handed him a ten and asked pointing my thumb over my shoulder at the stage, "Who is this?"

"MOOKIE BLAYLOCK OR SOMETHING." He took my ten and handed me back five ones.

The singers voice was different. Not like me or you or Mina different, but his voice sounded folksy and bluesy at the same time and the way it stood against the music was raw.

I don't know the name of the song, but it was their last one of the night. The singer dropped the mic on the stage but the guitarist picked it up and thanked everyone for coming out.

I stood there, leaning on the bar, sipping my whiskey listening as the band took their gear off stage. A few minutes later another set of guys were setting up their instruments with the sound tech.

Music was playing over the P.A. System but it was definitely quieter than the live band.

I turned to the bartender and asked, "The guy who does your flyers, is he around?"

"Cory? You like his work or hate it?" The bartender asked.

"I might have some freelance work for him, I'm a promoter," I lied.

The guy laughed, "Right."

I drank the last of my whiskey, put it down then pointed at the glass.

"He probably owes you money." The bartender refilled my drink.

I put a twenty down on the bar and said, "Keep the change."

"He helps clean up at the end of the night. Probably getting stoned out back," the barman said as he took the bill.

It was a short break between sets and the next band started up so I turned to watch leaning on my elbows on the bar. Since I was there I might as well enjoy my watered down whiskey and do a little people watching. Hunting this mosquito wasn't my priority on this trip but if this Cory and the blood sucker were one in the same, I'd find out at some point either at the end of the night or maybe come back and stake the place out another night if necessary.

That was when I heard Jerry Cantrell's guitar coupled with Layne Staley's voice for the first time.

The band looked like they were homeless, probably were, but they were suited to perform together. There was this sound in the singers voice that seemed like a bunch of broken pieces held together buy the guitar and drums and bass.

I stood there, sucked in for their first three songs.

Then the bartender tapped me on the shoulder. He pointed to a guy standing near a side door.

"Cory," the bartender yelled.

I nodded to the bartender, but didn't move. I wanted to listen to the music for a bit longer and now I knew what the kid looked like.

But then I saw a girl walk toward the side door and Cory opened it for her. She turned and smiled at Cory and generally in my direction.

For a moment, just a flash really, I felt like I was looking at eyes I hadn't seen in almost 400 years. A little like mine and a lot like my wife's.

That was when I caught the twitch.

That subtle shift in Cory's face when you know those things smell someone they just need to eat. Someone they just can't resist.

"Fuck,"I said to myself and finished off my whiskey. I dropped the glass on the bar.

"Another?" The bartender asked.

"No," I said. "What's the name of this band?"

"Alice In Chains," he yelled as he took the glass away and turned to another guy at the bar.

I spun on my heel and headed toward the side door. Cory was already out there with this girl.

Before I headed outside, I looked back at the stage and listened for a few more seconds.

I took a deep breath and headed through the door.

Outside I could see the girl walking, poorly, down the sidewalk away from the club.

Walking next to her, Cory looked to be offering to help keep her steady.

The problem was I could only hear one heart beating between the two and it wasn't Cory's.

I weighed my options, and if I even wanted to bother getting involved.

But then you and Mina's stupid voices came into my head going on and on about the balance that's keeps the world spinning the right way on its axis.

And if I randomly read an article in the paper and got a bad feeling about it, then that means the police would start getting asked tough and unanswerable questions. That kind of publicity was never good for humanity and always worse for my kind.

I sighed and jumped up on top of the building.

Cory didn't hear me as he was fixated on the girl and she wouldn't have been able to hear me even if she wasn't hammered.

I could smell him now.

She could too, that was obvious by the smile on her face.

I've never met a woman who didn't light up the moment she smelled lavender. And this lavender was spiked with magic.

I followed along on the roof tops of two or three buildings before I lost my high ground and had to go back to the street to continue following them.

She was giggling from whatever he was whispering to her. I could hear him at the time, but don't remember what he was saying. I do remember thinking that whatever he was saying wouldn't have worked on any woman if he didn't smell intoxicating.

But he had her attention and guided her into an alley on the next block.

The streets were empty, that part of Seattle was a cesspool at that time, might still be, I haven't been back there in a long time. But no one wanted to be on those streets at that time of night. Or really in the day for that matter.

That was going to be my chance, as he was about to take his.

I stepped into the alley behind them and said, "Hey Cory."

Cory spun the girl around, she let out a small yelp, but he covered her mouth with one hand and wrapped his other arm around her like a vice.

His face was very different now. His mouth was wider with fangs making it impossible for himself to close it properly.

"You're terrible at this Cory," I said, inching further into the alley. "Whoever made you made a shitty mosquito. You've already attracted the wrong kind of attention. We don't tolerate that."

"I'm gonna kill you next," Cory said, "whatever you are."

Cory reared his head back then came down with all of his jagged, yellow teeth toward the girls neck.

Luckily for me I carry a knife everywhere I go. Usually a couple of knives. And fire. Still have the zippo Matilda gave me after World War II. Had to have the internals replaced but Zippo is pretty great about that and its covered for the life of the lighter. Don't think they had my lifetime in mind for that policy though.

I was able to get the folder I keep in my pocket out and in the split second before his fangs buried into that poor girls flesh, I threw it knowing I couldn't close the distance between us fast enough. The blade found its mark in the back of his throat and he stumbled back letting out a blood curdling, guttural scream. The blade poked out the back of his neck and his mouth was filled by the handle

The girl screamed too.

I jumped over her head and landed behind her putting myself between them.

"Run," I yelled and she bolted.

Cory yanked my knife out of his mouth, his own congealed blood and spit covering my knife. He lunged for me - all teeth and knife coming at me.

When I had jumped over the girl, I had pulled the knife I had strapped around my ankle out. I side stepped Cory, buried that knife in the back of the blood suckers neck and kept driving down slamming his face and chest on the concrete.

Bones and cement cracked as the blade stuck out his neck and struck the ground.

I yanked toward myself and the blade ripped out the side of his neck.

Another scream, but this one was wet and came from a deeper place than his mouth as most of Cory's neck was gone.

I needed the rest of it to be gone, so in one smooth motion I came to my feet and kicked into the wound I just created in the side of his neck as hard as I could.

Every bone in my foot broke, but Cory's head rolled away from his body coming to a stop against a dumpster.

I stood still for a moment, listening as my foot healed itself. Bones cracked and crunched and groaned as they mended inside the flesh inside my shoe.

The girl was still running three blocks away now and no one else was around.

I opened the dumpster, tossed Cory's head and body in. Luckily I'm me and as long as I concentrated I could still hear the band from my little hobo fire.

Chapter 16

"When was the last time you spoke with Penny?" Hank asked staring into the fire and opening the Zippo.

"Same day you saw her last," Nick said. He sat up slowly and swung his legs over the edge of the hammock toward the fire. "But she met up with Suzy and Mina's cousins a few months ago in Greece, only in bird form though. But they knew it was her. It would be nice if she would visit us, even just as a bird."

"It would be," Hank said. He spun the flint wheel on the lighter and the flame came to life. Then he drained the beer he was holding with his other. He dropped the bottle in the pile he was making and it clattered with the others. Hank reached for another beer and flicked the cap off into the fire with his thumb. The little flame still dancing on the end of the Zippo in his left hand.

"The reason a true shapeshifter like her are thought of as myths is because so many of them prefer to be something else rather than human," Nick said watching Hank closely.

"I know that," Hank said closing the lighter extinguishing the flame.

"We could try and track her down. We are quite good at that."

"No, I promised her I would let her be everything she wants to be. So few beings get to go the direction she has chosen."

"It's okay to miss her." The click of the lighter snapping open rang between crackles from the camp fire.

"I know," Hanks said and took a sip of his beer.

"It's also good to talk to someone about missing her. Or anyone else you might miss."

"I know." A muffled snap came from Hank's left fist.

"Alright, I get it, that was you talking about it," Nick said and leaned back on the hammock. "Let's talk about something else."

Hank's jaw was clenched and his face was like a statue, his eyes trained on the fire, unblinking.

"What's the weirdest job you've ever had?" Nick asked. He was looking up at the stars again.

"You've run out of good prompts haven't you?"

"I'm curious if there is anything that would be considered odd or out of place on your resume considering the careers you've already mentioned in this conversation."

"I collected unicorn semen for medicinal purposes in Eastern Europe after I gave up pirating," Hank said.

"Seriously?" Nick sat up.

"No."

"Is that a thing though?"

"I don't know," Hank said. "Do Unicorns even exist?"

"I don't know actually. Seriously though, what's the oddest job you've ever had? Something has to pop out even to you amongst all the shit you've done for money."

"I can't think of anything odd," Hank said. "Try something else."

"Tell me about the night you were cursed?"

Hank narrowed his eyes at Nick, and growled, "I was a trapper for a while."

"Mink or beaver?"

"Neither," Hank said. "Splinter Cat and Hidebehind."

"What the hell are those?

"That's right, both are basically extinct here now."

"Here? As in the Americas?"

"More like I don't think they were exactly natives of our world."

Angry Chair
Canadian Territory - Late 1780's or early 90's

Splinter Cats looked like a Tabby Cat for the most part, but with a really big, thick skulled head. It used that head to ram trees trying to knock other animals and beehives out. It especially liked to eat raccoons - I personally think it had something to do with their thumbs - can't trust a creature with a thumb. It would eat the whole beehive; the bees, the hive, the wax and the honey.

Weird little creatures.

Their fur had the ability to camouflage them against anything. The were born with an invisibility cloak.

The big ones could splinter a tree like a bolt of lightning hence the name. Sounded like thunder too.

Usually, they just knocked an animal or two and some leaves out of the tree, ate quickly and disappeared to wherever they go. And I don't just mean they were good at hiding. After they finished eating they literally disappeared.

It's method of hunting had its drawbacks though and the creatures were always dealing with headaches that left them in a foul mood. And the only way to catch them was when they were invisible about to ram a tree. You had to wack them on the neck where their skull and neck meet. And you had to hit them hard, really, really hard.

Harder than a typical person could.

Hard enough that even I didn't always catch one.

If you went after it before it could eat it disappeared as well, or it rammed you to death.

Then it would eat you too.

I don't actually know what year it was, sometime in either the late 1780's or early 90's.

It doesn't really matter.

The Hudson Bay Company controlled most of the fur trade with some smaller trade groups operating on the fringe or directly controlled by the British anyway, so they might as well have been the Hudson.

Most of the fur trade revolved around beaver, but there were dozens of animals people trapped for profit. And a select few people dealt in more rare and often supernatural pelts like the Splinter Cat and the Hidebehind. Those two were the main ones hunted here in North America. The clientele were very specific for those furs because of the price.

And the fact that so few people even knew they existed. But when The Hudson Bay found out about them, they scoured the globe for someone to hunt them.

That was where guys like me came in.

From what I learned there had only been three others that successfully ever killed one.

A bunch of mortals and a few other supernatural creatures had tried, and failed.

There was one story where a group of men went after one, tried to kill it while visible, and it ate three of them. The fourth got away and went on record with his story.

A man, Robert Davis, approached me from The Hudson Bay Company asking odd questions, I was suspicious but intrigued because I could smell he wasn't human but didn't know what he was. Never actually found out because he left on an expedition into the Northwest Territories and never returned.

When I met him though he handed me sheet of paper that gave instructions on how to hunt and kill a Splinter Cat. It was written by a man named Timothy Scott.

Mr. Davis told me that Mr. Scott was a special kind of hunter, and that he had survived multiple encounters with the Splinter Cat and was the first to successfully get a usable pelt.

Sadly though, after a few years of this work he went missing while out in the wilderness.

I suspected he was like me and after a few years he either got bored or got too close to someone and took off after a disastrous incident. I never found out what exactly he was, nor have I had any luck tracking him down, but I suspect he was possibly Were Bear or a Were Elephant. That would explain his ability to track the cats and kill them.

Not every werecreature is as strong as I am, and there are some that are stronger. However there aren't any that I have found that can smell quite as well as I can. And this gave me the opportunity to make a lot of money while staying very far away from other people for a good chunk of time.

It was amazing.

I could track the Splinter Cats while they were invisible because of their scent. It was subtle, and it's hard to track something that is invisible but almost impossible when they don't leave tracks and barely have a scent.

And that's why people wanted their furs.

It made the best invisibility cloaks money could buy, the only one really.

But you had to kill and skin the Splinter Cat while it was invisible to get the benefits.

I was a few hundred miles north of the Great Lakes, no idea really where, and I had been tracking a Splinter Cat for over a month.

Got a little sidetracked during the full moon.

I was right on the little guy's tail as it started to make its run at this tree.

But the wind shifted and just before I could strike, it turned on me and buried its hard head right in my gut.

Sent me flying through the forest, taking out branches as thick as my thigh until I slammed into a massive oak tree.

I gasped for breath and panicked trying to catch the cat's scent in the air hoping it had just disappeared rather than have it stalking toward me about to ram me to death.

If that was even possible.

But it hadn't disappeared.

I could actually see it, which was way more dangerous, and it was walking slowly toward me.

These creatures were beautiful. They have turquoise eyes and their fur shimmers between emerald, gold and sky blue. Honestly, it's mesmerizing. but I hadn't ever really given it a second thought, until I figured it was about to kill me.

MOTHER RED CAP! That was the name of Jimmy's club in Chicago. That came out of nowhere.

Anyway, the cat was mesmerizing. It came over and sat down looking me right in the eye.

"Why you kill us?" It more or less hissed. A side effect of not having a human mouth or pallet.

I didn't know these fuckers could talk. I had only ever heard them hiss and howl and do their little roars. "Since when can you guys talk?"

"You kill us, we learn," the cat said.

Evolution wasn't really something people knew about at that time. I don't think Darwin had even been born yet.

"Guess you're gonna kill me now?" I said finally catching my breath.

It sort of shrugged its shoulders as much as a cat could.

"Is there something else I can do for you then?" I said and pushed myself to my feet.

"Why you kill us?" It asked again.

"Seriously?" I said. "Your fur, people use it to make themselves invisible like you can."

The Splinter Cat cocked its head to the side and narrowed it eyes and said, "Bad hunters, take our gifts."

"Basically," I said.

"We know you," the cat said. "You kill much of us."

"I have trapped quite a few of you," I said.

"Too many," it said and jumped up on my shoulder and turned on its cloak.

To make an invisibility cloak out of the Splinter Cat's fur you needed a few of them to make it big enough. I had only been trapping them for three or four years, but I knew of at least twelve cloaks that existed from furs I had personally caught.

I had worn one before and it's an odd feeling to say the least. Like walking into a spiders web.

I felt that odd feeling when the cat went stealth, and looked down at my hands. I couldn't see them or the rest of me.

"You can make people invisible just by touching them?"

"Yes," the animal said. I felt its tail twitch around my face and the end of it brushed my upper lip.

"And why do I care?" I asked.

The animal jumped down from my shoulder looked up at me and shrugged.

"Where do you go when you aren't hunting?" I asked. "That's the only time anyone has ever seen one of you."

"Home," the cat said. "I go, no come back. Tree bears and sweet hive not worth."

"You come here for the raccoons and the honey from where?" I asked.

"Home," it said.

"And where is that?" I asked again hoping for something , anything more.

"Not here," the cat said.

It was like talking to a teenager.

"Are you going to come back?" I asked trying to see if I could possibly figure out when It would come back so I could pick up the hunt.

"No," It said and disappeared.

That was the last time I saw one of them and from what I've heard it was the last time anyone ever saw one. Can't even see their furs as the cloaks are still invisible.

As for the Hidebehind, I'm pretty sure we just killed them all. Those things were dumb.

Chapter 17

"That was only slightly odd, more sad," Nick said. His fingers were laced behind his head on the hammock. "But now I want a talking cat. Thanks for ruining my chances by hunting it until it figured out the restaurant was bad for their survival."

"Did you not hear a word I said?" Hank asked and pointed at Nick with the end of his beer bottle. "Those little creatures were mean and one of the hardest things I have ever tried to kill."

"I didn't say I wanted a stuffed one," Nick said.

"You couldn't catch the buggers. Tried it. Only way to get them like I said was when they were about to strike the tree while they were invisible and you had to kill it."

"Like you said you never tried to talk to it. Leads me to believe no one had. You and everyone else went straight for the kill rather than try another tactic. Archaic reasoning. Its different but I want what it has, KILL IT!"

"It's in every living creatures nature to kill for what it wants if necessary."

"If that's true how do you explain the last 30ish years?"

"I haven't killed anyone recently only because of the help you and Mina have given me all these years."

"Don't forget about Gert and Penny."

"You know what I mean. And none of us have seen Penny in five years, so I would say she is as helpful as Gert who's dead."

"Are you trying to thank me in your own little way? Cause don't, over the course of this conversation killing you has crossed my mind many times."

"I know. I needed to tell you all of this so that you can make that choice."

"You think I need more information to want to kill you? Idiot, I want to kill you every day for one reason or another. Knowing that you are doing your very best to control your curse and surrounding yourself with the people who can help you when you need it is more important than what you did in the past, intentionally or accidentally. You can't help people when you're dead."

"What happens when you die? I almost lost all control when Gert was killed, and you have become even more to me than she ever was."

"Stop being so soft."

"What if I asked Mina to end my life for me? Would she grant me that wish."

"Probably," Nick said. "But Suzy, you know your God daughter, would probably put me and Mina in the worst old folks home she could find if Mina executed you. And Adam would never speak to us again, not that he talks to us much these days. Kid thinks he knows everything and I just want to go Homer Simpson on him every once in a while."

"You were the same way at that age. Kid probably knows more than both of us though with these annoying smart phones and all."

"So, my point is you'll have another generation of Stantons to help you. Suzy is still able to turn into whatever she wants into her twenties. You know how rare that is with Penny being the only one you have ever met. And whomever Adam wakes the power in as his life mate, will most likely help you with some encouragement from him and his sister. Unless said person kills you before they can convince them you're not as much of a dick as you let on."

"Glad to hear I might have the support of your children with my affliction in the future. Give me another prompt, something else to talk about."

"Tell me about the night you were cursed."

The clank from the lighter in Hank's left hand opening cut through the air.

Hank sat there for a moment, staring at the fire gritting his teeth.

The fire spat as the heat found a pocket of moisture or half rotted knot in the wood. Embers shot into the sky above but Hank's eyes didn't leave the dancing flames.

"Never mind," Nick said and sat up on the hammock. He threw his legs over the edge and dug his toes into the grass.

It was damp and Nick looked out toward the tree line to the East. A glow was creeping up through the horizon.

"I made a mistake."

The lighter snapped shut and Nick snapped back to attention. He eased back into the hammock, his feet letting go of the Earth.

Hank stared into the flames. His jaw clenched, he breathed in slowly, out even slower letting his face soften.

"I knew the witch was taking my pigs. She'd been doing it for years but I had looked the other way. Whether or not she took my daughter is irrelevant at this point. I should have put a stop to the witch taking my pigs the first instance. If she did take my daughter, it was because I had turned a blind eye to her behavior and she felt emboldened. Or I was just wrong and something else happened and I sentenced that woman to death. Either way it was my fault."

The two men sat for a moment and the fire danced between them. Hank's eyes locked on the flames and Nick's were trained on Hank's face.

Hank looked Nick in the eye. "I was her father, it was my job to protect her and I failed. What happened doesn't even matter after all this time. And I don't want an answer anymore, its better not knowing I think. I hired what was supposed to be the greatest medium to ever live and she turned out to be a charlatan. They always are. You and Mina are the closest thing to someone who can talk to the other side."

"But we can only see the other side of the curtain in this world. What comes next is as much a mystery to us as it is to everyone else," Nick said quietly.

The fire crackled and spat embers into the darkness above with a trailing hiss.

"I know the names of two of your daughters," Nick said, "but your oldest, you've never told me her name."

"Her name was Hannah."

Over Now
Kelsey Town - 1701

It had rained most of that day.

I had been working from before sun up to supper time on the furthest part of the farm from the main house digging out rock. I had spent months clearing more land so that I could have room to rotate crops.

I had missed supper as the rain weighed me down and made the work drag by, but decided to give up as I wanted to have some light to put away the tools and clean up.

I came back dragging only half of my tools with me as my muscles rebelled at that final chore. And I just wanted to see my girls and tell the youngest two, Abigail and Elizabeth, a bed time story.

As I was dragging the tools to the barn, I saw Hannah tugging a basket filled with stale bread, apple cores, corn cobs and other table scraps though the muck.

Her cloak covered most of her small frame, but mud climbed up her little legs with every step. The hood of her cloak fell back as she struggled a bit with the basket in the muck. Everything was grey and wet except her bright eyes and blue silk ribbon holding her hair back.

The pigs foraged much of the day all over the property, often times finding ways through fences I had around crops - pigs are smart buggers - but we also brought out most of our scraps to them. They are what we had instead of garbage disposals and before we really figured out how to compost.

As soon as Hannah could walk she would help me bring the pigs their nightly treat of slop. And as soon as she was big enough to drag the bins and baskets we used to bring it out to them, she wanted the chore.

I loved that about her, she wasn't afraid of working, she wasn't afraid of getting dirty.

I walked into the barn to put my tools away.

Hannah was tossing the left-overs a few pieces at a time over the fence, lightening the basket as she would until she could lift and dump it over into the pen.

"Hi daddy!" Hannah squealed and smiled at me. "Don't worry, we saved some supper for you too."

"I was very concerned that you may have forgotten about my grumbling belly as the four of you laughed and ate without me," I smiled. "Would you like some help with that?"

"I have it daddy," she said. "Go in and dry off and quiet that belly."

"Give a holler if you need help," I said and smiled as I headed back toward the house.

I could hear the pigs rustling and oinking and eating as Hannah tossed more scraps into the pen even over the sloppy sounds my wet feet made in the mud.

It was only drizzling at this point, and as I got to the back door something to my left caught my attention. Something moving quickly, and oddly.

I turned and looked out toward my fields to the West. The sun was setting but still shining through the trees turning the sky orange at the horizon. It was the Witch that lived out in the woods a few miles from my property. She turned and looked directly at me. She had a sack slung over her shoulder with something inside squirming.

I looked to the barn behind me, but didn't see Hannah, I only saw the basket overturned in the mud with the last of the scraps soaking up the brown water.

The pigs were still oinking and squealing and eating as they had a moment ago. Maybe a bit more so possibly because I was yelling or the witch had just taken Hannah.

"Hannah?" I said but there was no response from the barn.

Then I yelled, "HANNAH!"

Still nothing and I looked back to the Witch who was now walking away into the woods on the other side of the field. The bag over her shoulder squirmed and writhed on her back.

I took off after her and screamed, "HANNAH!"

But I couldn't close the distance between the Witch and me. No matter how hard I pumped my legs. One moment she would look like she was maybe 50 feet ahead of me, then poof she'd be hundreds of feet ahead. I would start closing the gap and boom she'd be hundreds of feet ahead again. Like when you watch those time lapse videos from a robbery at a gas station and its all jumpy because its recording at one frame per second rather than smoothly at thirty frames a second.

After ten minutes of running through the underbrush, my face scratched, my lungs burning and my legs weighed down with mud, I lost her.

She just vanished.

At first I couldn't rationalize her just being there, ahead of me and then the next just being gone. She hadn't outrun me, she couldn't of hidden behind anything as there were no trees wider than a child and she hadn't taken a turn. She simply disappeared completely this time.

I decided to head up to the road rather than continue in the brush, and pick up the path out to her cabin. It was the only place I could think of that she would go, the only place she might take my Hannah.

But when I got there, my lungs on fire, hell my whole body was on fire and steam rose off of me like a piece of green wood, there was no one there.

Back then, Chatfield Hollow wasn't a State Park. There wasn't a beach around a pond but only a meandering brook running through the ridges.

I headed down to the brook thinking maybe she would come up from there having followed it back from the road. And when I say road I mean a path big enough for a horse and carriage to snake though the woods.

Again I found nothing and the rain and the darkness was making it impossible to find any trace of anyone or anything going through there that day.

She could be making her way up to any one of the many ridges that encircle the area. Any of the small caves that dot the hills. Or somewhere no one even knew about in those woods that the Witch had made or dug out or just stumbled upon.

I ran to the few small caves I knew about on the southern ridge line, but found nothing.

I headed back to her cabin but it was still empty.

This time though, I didn't just look quickly inside the one room hut. I went inside and checked the fire place first. There was no fire, but the coals still held heat and I hovered my hands over them as I realized how numb they were and how much they were shaking.

The door opened behind me, but before I had time to turn around or brace myself an animal slammed into me.

The squealing and the feel of its flesh as I got a hold of it gave away that it was a pig. On my knees I pushed it away and the hog ran toward a corner of the room searching for something to hide under.

A bit of light was coming in from the now open door and a figure appeared in the frame.

Then there as a flash from the hands of the figure in the doorway, the air sizzled and the room was so bright my eyes burned. For a moment or two I didn't feel anything but then it hit me. It was like bugs crawling all over my skin. I fell to hands and all of my muscles were tense, contracted and strained.

And then it was dark again.

Totally black after the blinding flash.

I could hear shuffling around me, but couldn't place where it was coming from.

And breathing. Old, labored, wheezy and whistling breaths that sounded and felt wet.

I forced myself to stand. I reached my hands out slowly searching the darkness for whoever was in the room with me but I found nothing. That feeling of bugs crawling up my spine came over me and my body stiffened.

There was no flash this time. I fell forward straight out the door of the small cabin into the mud and the moss.

"Hannah, where is Hannah?" I mumbled as my face hit the dirt outside the entry way.

I couldn't move. But I could feel someone kneel down next to me. I could smell her and her rancid, hot, wet breath as she whispered into my ear, "How would I know."

I wanted nothing more than to tear her to pieces, but my body wasn't following my thoughts. My hands only twitched as I laid there.

I groaned as I could still feel the Witch's hot breath next to my ear.

Then I screamed. A blood curdling, primitive, hate filled scream.

My reaction startled the Witch and she jumped back. She scrambled back into her hut and slammed the door.

That feeling of pins and needles after your arm or leg falls asleep erupted over my entire body. More like knives and daggers really. The pain shot me to my feet and I couldn't fight the instinct to run.

I was on my property before I could gain enough control of myself to stop, but I couldn't bring myself to turn back and face her again.

Not alone.

I ran to my horse barn, grabbed a saddle and dressed my fastest mare as quickly as I could.

With the commotion I made, my wife came outside with a lantern.

"What is going on Henry? Where have you been and where is Hannah?" she asked. "I found the basket over turned in the mud next to the pig pen."

"Please go inside. I think the Witch took Hannah and I'm going to get help. I tried…" I said but couldn't finish the thought, my miserable failure.

"Ride fast, Henry," my wife said as I jumped on the mare and took off for town.

It wasn't hard rallying folks to help me. The basics were enough to incite their fears and prejudices of the witch. I can't really remember that part though. It was a blur. My anger and my fear and my anxiety were so potent that it is hard to remember anything other than the feelings.

It was outside of the Witch's cabin that everything slowed down. It was well past midnight at that point, but her spells were keeping us at bay.

Some folks had brought muskets and they fired into the cabin, but the shot stopped just short of impact and fell to the mud.

A few others stormed the front door but couldn't even get to the handle.

Most tried to hack at the door or the walls or the windows with whatever farm tool they could find at that time of night but none of them made any headway.

As the mob's frustration grew, someone tossed a lantern at the hut. The lantern itself bounced off the barrier surrounding the building, but the fire, the fire cut right through. It landed on the thatched roof and the flames caught instantly. Her spells seemed to be useless against the fire and the others with lanterns and torches all tossed theirs onto the pyre. The town folk screamed and hollered and cheered as the flames overtook the house in a matter of seconds.

I screamed and rushed the cabin but was grabbed by three strong men who knew there was no hope of me getting in there let alone getting Hannah out if she was inside.

That is when we heard the cackling from inside the cabin. The etherial, other worldly incantation came next from inside. Then the squealing of a pig.

The burning inside my bones came right as the squealing stopped. And it quickly spread to my muscles and then my skin and a scream like I have never heard escaped my throat. Guttural, bloody and so terrifying the three men holding me let go and backed away along with the rest of the mob.

I dropped to my knees, my scream continued even though my lungs were empty, and something else screamed while I sucked a breath in.

I fell to my stomach in the moss and the mud and the ash that was falling all around us from the burning hut. It was so bright. And hotter than any fire I had ever seen.

And I continued to scream as the towns folk who had marched there with me, who had lit the cabin on fire, possibly with my Hannah inside, slinked away into the darkness, away from the fire, away from the carnage, away from the terrible sound coming from me.

I woke up there a little after dawn.

Alone.

The only thing left standing was the stone fireplace and chimney. I crawled into the rubble, still glowing embers burning my hands and my shirt and my pants and my boots, and I laid back on the smoldering ash wondering if my daughter had just been burned alive.

The Ballad of Hank Kelsey

Killer Is Me

Coda
Don't Follow
Kelsey Town, 2059

The cemetery was still, even with so many creatures standing around the casket as it slowly descended into the ground.

The grave stone read 'STANTON' across the top and below it were Nick and Mina's names. She had passed a few months before, at the ripe old age of 88. Nick followed a few days ago from a mixture of heartbreak and cancer.

As with most funerals, black was the fashionable choice, Hank included. His black suit was covered by an over coat hanging down to his ankles as he stood with Nick and Mina's children to say a final goodbye.

The stand out was a young girl, no bigger than five and the spitting image of her grandmother Mina at that age, wearing an array of color. A bright Gorton Fisherman style rain hat, a purple raincoat, red pants and rainbow Wellies.

The little girl, Moira, stood between Hank while her mother Suzie and her father stood to her right, both with tears streaming down their face.

The little girl reached up and took Hank's hand.

Slowly, Hank looked down at the tiny hand in his and smiled.

Grinning through her tears Moira said, "Its all right to cry but they are okay, Grandpa told me so. And Hannah, she told me she's okay too and to tell you it wasn't anyone's fault, especially not the pigs. They were just hungry, they were always hungry."

Hank's eyes widened as he knelt down to eye level with the five year old. Everything from that fateful day three hundred and fifty eight years ago came into focus in his turbulent mind. The missing pieces fitting together finally after so much time and so much anger and so much pain. Moira's smile grew even bigger as she put her hand on Hanks' cheek and a torrent of tears ran down over her fingers.

The Golden Thread Of Henry Kelsey

1674

Henry Kelsey Born April 19th

1684

Hank's brother Joseph leaves home to fight in the second Indian War.

1701

Hank's daughter goes missing, he convinces town it was a witch. The townsfolk have themselves a good ol'fashion witch hunt and burn her shack to the ground, with the witch inside. Hank is cursed by her to suffer as a Werepig for instigating the whole thing.

1702

While on business in Nantucket, Hanks meets Benjamin Pike, a Werelobster, after accidentally killing Samuel Bishop, the first casualty of his curse.

1711

Charles Henry Kelsey born, Hank's first grandson who he and his wife convinced the world was his because his daughter got knocked up by a town Selectman during an affair.

1775, April 19th

Hank fights at the first battle of the Revolutionary War in Lexington and Concord.

1781

Looking for adventure, Hank becomes a Pirate Captain and sets sail for the Caribbean.

1780's or 90's

Hank works for The Hudson Bay Company hunting Hidebehinds and Splinter Cats for their furs.

1836

While preparing to travel the Oregon Trail, Hank is forced to flee Independence Missouri after accidentally killing his fiancé Lucy Devereux, her father and their servant.

1849

Living in San Francisco, Hank meets a woman named Josephine who turns out to be a Werewolf. They end up burning San Francisco to the ground.

1863

As part of the Union Army, while on patrol outside Chancellorsville, Virginia, Hank stumbles across Lt. Gen. Stonewall Jackson and helps the general part ways with his arm.

1921

At the beginning of Prohibition Hank bootlegged Hard Cider from his apple orchard to keep himself busy until, inevitably, something terrible happened.

1945

Hank helps an Australian Spy named Matilda off of a Japanese Battle Ship. The information she brings back to the allies helps end WWII. And they have a love affair that goes horribly wrong. Hank inadvertently helps a young Australian country singer write the biggest hit of his career because of it all.

1956

Hank ends up in Vegas Hustling poker and befriends Frank Sinatra and happens to save his life during a botched hit by some Mobsters.

1986

Hank unintentionally helps awaken the power within Nick Stanton and Mina Medellin, setting off the events chronicled in The Ballad of Nick & Mina.

1990, October 22

Hank hunts down a vampire and stumbles upon Pearl Jam's first ever show, as Mookie Blaylock, when they opened for Alice In Chains.

1996

The Great Comet of 1996, Comet Hyakutake, passed by Earth in March of that year. Hank and Mina attend the Tournament held in Vegas between Supernatural creatures on a year with the appearance of a great comet. Mina befriends Asterion the Minitour and learns a great deal about the other women who have held her position throughout the ages.

2018

While telling Nick his life story, Hank comes to admit that he, as Hannah's father, is at fault for her disappearance. He should have protected her, he should have kept her safe. And he has had to live with that feeling for hundreds of years.

2059

At Nick's funeral, his granddaughter Moira takes Hank's hand and delivers a message from Hank's daughter Hannah beyond the veil.

Acknowledgements

I need to first and foremost thank my wife, Claire. She has lived with me and Hank for our entire relationship and hasn't kicked either of us out.

To Chelsea and Marissa, I am forever grateful that you helped me workshop this book when this isn't even remotely in the wheel house of what you enjoy reading. Thank you!

Thank you to The Henry Carter Hull Library Creative Writing Group for giving me a space to read most of Hank's story out loud, to see what worked and what fell flat and indulge me in my experiment of writing a fictional memoir for an almost four hundred year old Werepig.

Scott, what can I say, without your relentless push this story would have never seen the light of day. Thank you for all the late nights at Burger King after we got kicked out of coffee shops and it was too cold for us to sit outside. Thank you, thank you, thank you.

Afterword

Hank Kelsey, the long lived Werepig, first appeared on paper in 2009 in The Pen & The Sword - the first book in my young adult trilogy The Ballad of Nick & Mina. But that isn't where he, or this whole universe started. It all started on a bench back in 1986 as my sister and I watched Halley's Comet pass close enough to our world for us to witness on our families little farm. I was five, and my father had just died. I didn't really understand death at that age, but I knew that those two events would impact my life in meaningful ways. When I started writing stories down, the idea of Halley's Comet hurtling past Earth was always on the fringe of my mind. I knew I wanted to use that event, and all the feelings and emotions it churned up for me, in a story. Hank Kelsey wasn't named then, nor did I have a vision of a Werepig, but the idea of being moved by the sight of that celestial event, it took hold of me and marked that life would forever be different. Much like it did for Hank when he met Nick & Mina, and became a part of their family.

After hearing the song *Killer Is Me* by Alice In Chains (only recorded for their MTV Unplugged performance, but not included in the broadcast) I felt the need to tell the back story of this long lived Werepig. Like many Science Fiction and Fantasy stories, this also gave me a platform to explore and write about societal issues such war, PTSD, addiction, masculinity (toxic and otherwise) and the unfathomable pain that comes with the loss of a child. Most of Hank's trauma and scars are hidden below the surface, but they are there, wreaking havoc in his world, as they do to many of us, no matter how well those wounds are dressed or how deep we have buried the resulting damage.

Jonathon Wolfer grew up in a small town on the shoreline of Connecticut. He's lived in New York, Los Angeles, & Las Vegas but calls the Lower Connecticut River Valley home these days. He loves Harleys, loves telling stories, loves hearing them and he loves the great outdoors.

For more about his work and what else he is up to visit

www.thelonewolfer.com